To Audrey

A Slip of the Tongue

and other short stories

Stefania Hartley

THE∗SICILIAN∗MAMA

ALSO AVAILABLE AS EBOOK
AND LARGE PRINT BOOK

Copyright © 2020 Stefania Hartley

ISBN: 979-8-6133-9876-8

Stefania Hartley asserts the moral right to be identified as the author of this work.

This is a work of fiction. Names, characters and events are solely the product of the author's imagination.

All the stories were first published in The People's Friend magazine.

To the real-life Tanino and Melina. I love you x

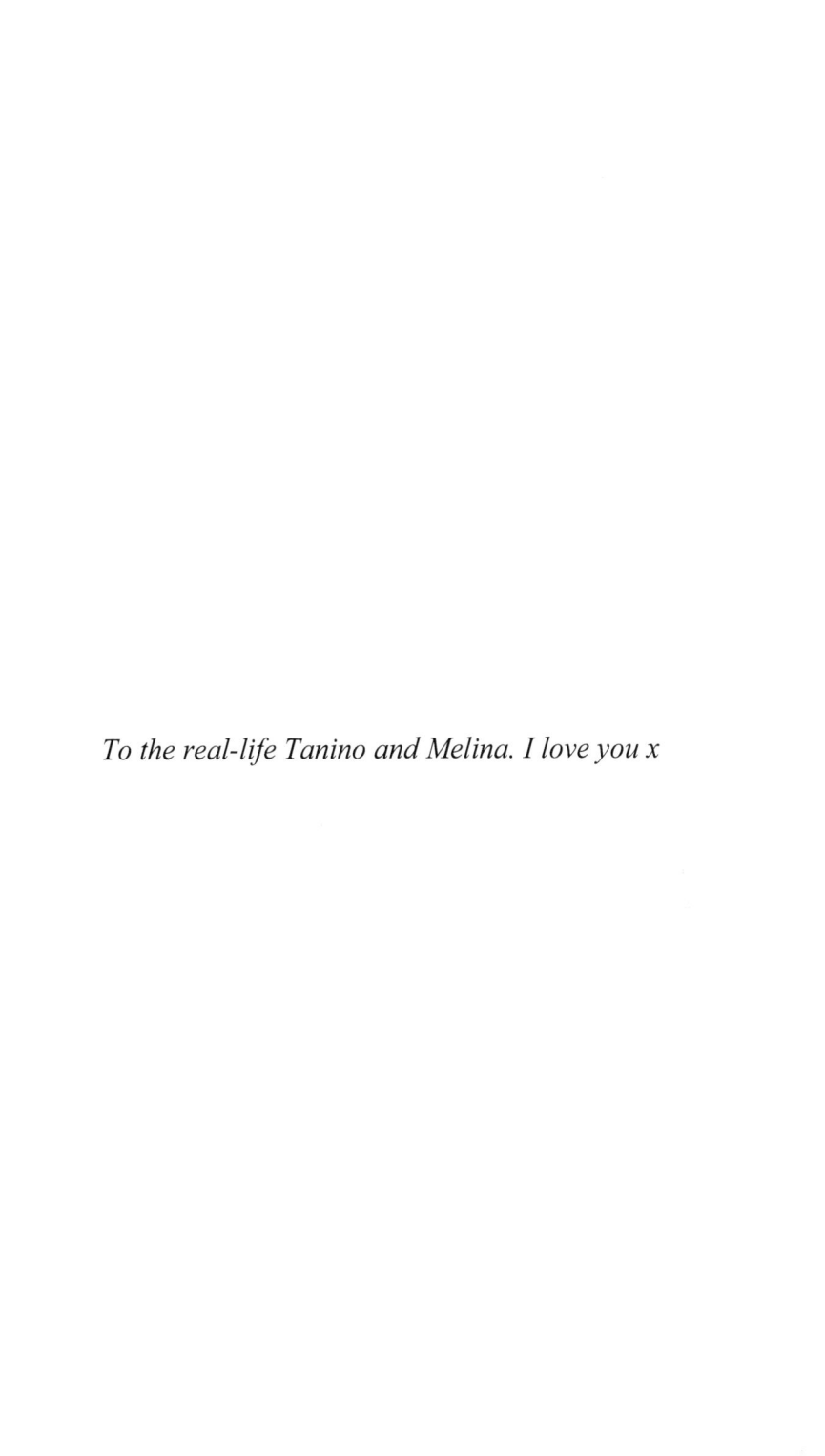

CONTENTS

1	Hot Gossip	1
2	The Carnival Party	8
3	Something for Supper	14
4	Swimming in Singapore	21
5	A Slip of the Tongue	32
6	Summer Loving	37
7	A Woman's Work	43
8	Lunch on St Lucy's Day	48
9	A Craftsman's Art	54
10	All the Way to America	60
11	A Class of their Own	65
12	Viewing Recommended	73
13	A Matter of Commitment	82
14	The Stolen Pisces	91
15	Once Bitten	101
	About the Author	108

1. HOT GOSSIP

Tanino held womankind in the highest regard, except for one thing: gossip. To him, anything from complaints about the weather to political slander was 'gossip'.

Melina was late coming home from church and Tanino had a pretty good idea why. Her lateness had started when Anna, one of Melina's church friends, had announced that her daughter was getting married. Tanino imagined the gaggle of women outside the church after evening Mass, gassing about flowers, wedding dresses and whatnot. Why did they love idle talk so much? Didn't they know that it was the work of the devil, that it led to gossip and gossip led to catastrophe?

What he most disliked about their chit-chat was that their husbands often were the object. He dreaded to imagine all that Melina's friends must know about him.

"I'm home!" Melina bounded through the door. She sounded breathless, which meant that she must have realized that she was late.

"It's because of that silly wedding that you're coming home late every evening, isn't it," he grumbled.

"Actually, no: we weren't talking about the wedding tonight." Melina dashed into the kitchen, turned on the oven and whipped her apron on. "We were talking about Anna's husband's hemorrhoid operations. The first one didn't go too well because—"

"I don't want to know!" Tanino covered his ears and made a mental note not to tell Melina if he ever suffered from embarrassing medical complaints.

Melina released the bread dough that was bursting through the gaps in the parcel she had brought from the bakery. Eagerly watching from the threshold, Tanino guessed that this must mean pizza tonight. She oiled a square baking tray, slapped the dough in and pushed it up to the corners, then opened a tin of tomatoes and sloshed them on top. She might as well have bought the pizza ready-made from the bakery if she was going to make it in such a hurry and with so little care. But he kept quiet because he was hungry.

"Did you know that Peppina's gone on holiday with her sister," Melina said with a hint of envy. "She's left her husband behind at home all alone."

Why was Melina telling him this? Did she too wish to go on holiday without her husband? "Rocco would have been much better company for her than her sister, if you ask me. Anyway, I'm not so sure that he will be staying 'at home all alone'." He winked.

These last words were simply meant as a joking threat, should Melina think of doing the same, but they grabbed Melina's attention by the throat. Her cheese-sprinkling stopped mid-air and she raised one eyebrow. "Do you know something that I don't?"

She sounded intrigued and a little resentful that Tanino might know a piece of information that she wasn't in on. Tanino had absolutely no idea what Rocco had planned for his time without his wife, but the chance to shock Melina and gain credit with her was irresistible for Tanino. "As a matter of fact," he breathed in importantly, "I do."

Melina wiped her hands on her apron and slammed the pizza into the lukewarm oven. "Tell me everything," she ordered.

"Nothing. It's just that Rocco is not going to be waiting like a puppy all alone in the apartment." Tanino floated out of the kitchen and Melina followed him to the door.

"Who is going to keep him company?"

Melina's curiosity was thicker than the cheese she had dropped on the pizza. "Not a woman, if that's what you're worried about."

She followed him into the corridor. "Are you involved?"

"I was invited, yes, of course. But I declined. Parties are not my thing." He continued to drift away, avoiding her gaze in case she read the bluff on his face. This made him look shifty and whipped Melina's excitement up to the maximum.

"Ah, it's a party then, is it?"

"Maybe."

"*Santo Cielo*, good Heavens, Peppina would never approve of that! They're going to leave an almighty mess in her home!"

Tanino did not fail to notice this description of their friends' marital home.

"When is it? Tonight?" Melina whispered conspiratorially.

"Maybe." Tanino's vagueness wasn't deliberate: he just hadn't worked out the details yet. But his sibylline answers had the desired effect on Melina. She was flushed with excitement, hopping from one slipper to the other.

"What time?"

"I can't tell you."

At this point, Tanino's fun abruptly came to an end. Instead of following him around the house, Melina scuttled to the phone. Oh no, she was going to tell her friends! He must call off his bluff before… before what? Melina embarrassed herself? *Ah.* That would teach her a lesson about the evil of gossiping, wouldn't it? He thought about it: as soon as her friends heard the fake news, they

3

would rush to their husbands and ask them if they were involved in the illicit party. Then it would become clear that Melina's information was a hoax. So Tanino let her make all the phone calls while he, instead, went to check on the pizza.

***

"I need Peppina's number immediately," Melina whispered into the phone.

"Why? What's happened?" Anna asked.

"I've just found out that her husband is giving a party in her house tonight."

"Oh dear. She won't like *that*."

"That's why I have to tell her."

"I'm sorry, but I don't have her cell number. I'm not even sure she's taken her phone with her. Try calling Rosaria, but first tell me more about the party."

"It's tonight. Just the men. They are bound to drink and play *scopone* into the night, if you ask me."

"Oh, my! I'd better check that Vincenzo isn't involved." At this point, they both quickly ended the call.

Melina called Rosaria.

"Sorry, Melina, I don't have Peppina's number but try Angela. First, tell me about this party!"

"Tonight. Men only. I bet they'll be drinking and gambling. I wouldn't be surprised if they watched unsuitable movies too."

There was a gasp at the other end of the phone, followed by silence. Then, "Betting, drinking, blue movies… oh dear! Do you know who's going?"

"Not my husband, of course. You'd better check on yours."

That call came to a swift end too. Eventually, Melina gave up on trying to contact Peppina. Enough people knew about the illicit party now, so surely somebody would pass the message on to her. She tottered to the kitchen and found Tanino sitting at the table, the pizza in the center with half missing already.

"I had to start without you. It was going cold," he muttered with his mouth full, blowing on the molten cheese.

She ate some pizza until the phone rang, when she jumped out of her chair and dashed to it.

"Valeria has tried Peppina's mobile but it's off. Nobody can get hold of her tonight," came Anna's voice from the other end. "By the time we speak to her, it'll be too late for her to stop the party. Should we just keep quiet and hope that Rocco clears up really well?"

Melina thought about it a little. "I would rather know, if I was her."

"I wouldn't."

"Then we all must meet and discuss what to do: we should all be on the same page. Call everyone and tell them to come to mine in half an hour."

"But there are the finals of *Ballando con le Stelle*, Dancing with the Stars, on TV tonight."

"We can watch it at mine. Tanino doesn't mind."

***

Rocco was eating stale bread with tinned tuna and watching *Commissario Montalbano* when the intercom rang. Who could it be at this time in the evening? Pinuccia returning early from her trip? He put down his plate and walked slowly over to the receiver. "Hello?"

"Let us in, you cheeky Judas. Let us in!"

Rocco didn't understand in what way he could possibly have betrayed his friend, but he recognized Vincenzo's voice and thought that it would be easier to understand him face-to-face so he buzzed him in.

Moments later the apartment doors burst open and Vincenzo, Mimmo, Fabrizio, Giovanni and Peppe tumbled in with parcels and bottles. The landing filled with the heavenly smell of hot *cannoli* cakes, pizza and other baked goods. "How dare you give a party and not invite us!" They slapped him on the back.

"I have no idea what you're talking about." They

glanced into his apartment, where the tuna panino was resting, sad and lonely, on the table. The TV showed a blonde flirting with stone-faced detective Montalbano.

"Is that what you call a 'blue movie', Rocco?" Everyone laughed except Rocco, who felt as confused as a knotted skein of wool.

"You just said all that so that people would come over!"

"Then he offers us a tuna panino!"

As they bantered, they all piled into his apartment. They sat around the TV devouring warm pizza and *cannoli* overflowing with sweet ricotta. They watched Montalbano expose the murderer instead of the blonde and then had a quick round of cards with Monopoly money, because their real cash had gone into buying the cakes and the wine.

At ten to ten, Vincenzo announced that it was time to go home before their wives returned from Melina and Tanino's: the silly dancing show would be finishing soon.

"Ah, that's why Tanino hasn't come with you: he's trapped at home with all the wives. Poor guy!" Rocco said. He had finally understood.

***

Tanino had hoped to watch his favorite TV serial, the one about detective Montalbano, but Melina had invited all her friends and they all wanted to watch the dancing. By the time he went to his usual café, he was desperate for male company. Luckily, Rocco was there.

"Hello, Rocco. Shouldn't you be having something more substantial, considering that your missus isn't cooking for you?" Tanino asked, looking at the tiny shot of espresso his friend was sipping.

"I'm on detox today. I ate too much sugar last night."

Tanino's ears pricked up. "What did you do last night?" he asked slowly.

"A few of the boys came to my house."

Tanino felt like his eyes were about to jump out of their orbits. Rocco's party was meant to be his fabrication, not a reality! "So you had a... party?"

"I wouldn't call it that: we just ate takeout pizza and *cannoli* and watched Montalbano."

No! They ate proper pizza and watched his favorite program, while he was stuck with *Ballando con le Stelle* and half the women in town.

"I'm sorry you couldn't come," Rocco said, perhaps moved by Tanino's reaction. "I understand that you were 'babysitting' the wives. But don't worry, we'll do it again next time Peppina goes away."

Still with his eyes bulging out of his head, Tanino swallowed his espresso, made his excuses and left before any more of his friends turned up to tell him how great a night he'd organized for them. Or who was the murderer in that Montalbano episode.

Back home, Melina was putting away her bags of shopping. "Tanino, you won't believe what I found!"

Oh please, no more gossip. He didn't reply. Melina tottered out of the kitchen with a grin and her hands tucked behind her back. "I was told by Rosaria who heard it from Angela that Valeria—"

"Please, no more gossip!"

"What gossip? Look here!" She pulled her arms out and thrust a box towards him. *Commissario Montalbano, the full series.* Tanino couldn't believe his eyes. A big smile stretched across his face.

"Oh, thank you!"

"You see, I was told by Rosaria who heard it from Angela that Valeria bought a half-price box at the newsagent's, so I went too. It was seventy per cent off, but only for today."

Tanino smiled. "I see now, dear: you don't gossip. You just share information." He winked and hugged her.

2. THE CARNIVAL PARTY

Not all our memories are real memories. Some are the results of the tales we've heard, the photos we've seen and the conversations we've had becoming integrated into our own memories to the point of feeling real.

But the story I'm about to tell you cannot be anything other than real, because my feelings for Alessio Filigrino were a secret that only I knew.

Alessio Filigrino sat behind me in our class at the *Istituto Sant'Agostino*. He had long eyelashes and a shy smile which always started in his soft hazel eyes. His round face rested on his neck like a daisy on a stalk in an adorably cute way. He didn't speak much and, when he did, it was mostly in whispers. But his eyes—hidden behind the fringe of his bob—spoke for him. As I spent only my first year of schooling in the *Istituto*, it must have been my fifth birthday when all this happened.

The date had fallen just before the beginning of Lent, when in Italy we celebrate Carnival, so my mother suggested that my birthday party could be a Carnival costume party. I loved the idea. When I proudly gave out the invitations to my class, I was delighted to find out that Alessio Filigrino was coming! Time to dress to impress.

I chose to dress up as a belly-dancing odalisque. Mamma and Grandma turned to a dubiously skilled seamstress who owned a shambolic shop of household items and a large talking macaw. Despite the woman's disappointing sartorial skills and the undeniable fact that the outfit didn't expose my midriff like that of a true belly-dancing odalisque, I was pleased with it: it was made of shiny golden fabric and rustled mysteriously when I moved. I was even more pleased with it—elated, even—when I heard through the class grapevine that Alessio Filigrino was dressing up as a sultan. (We had been reading the book One Thousand and One Nights in class after all.)

As my birthday cake was overloaded with chocolate shavings, so the party became inflated with my expectations: Alessio and I would dance together, engage in pleasant conversation, or just enjoy each other's company, because it was my birthday—and on birthdays, wishes come true.

But twenty-nine superheroes, princesses and TV celeb robots turned up to the party before my beloved sultan. By the time he finally made his appearance, the others were already jumping around to the beat of the Mazinger Z theme tune, high on Fanta and Sprite.

I don't remember Mrs. Filigrino's face—my worldview reached as far as adults' waists—but I remember that she said to her son, "Alessio, say happy birthday to Marta," and he mumbled something that might have been "happy birthday" and handed me a present. As soon as I had freed his hands from the parcel, he went back to clinging to his mother's hand. Oh, how I wished he had grabbed mine instead!

Eventually, his Mamma kissed him goodbye and was swallowed by the elevator. Alessio stood on the threshold, gazing at the revelers inside with an unsure expression. Maybe he didn't recognize his masquerading classmates. In hindsight, I should have taken his hand and led him inside, I should have shown him to the buffet table, told him, "try the *arancine* rice balls, they're my favorite" and filled him a plate and a cup, like a good host would do. But I didn't muster the courage in time.

"Alessio!" shouted his best friend from the other side of the crowded room, with a Spiderman mask hanging off one of his ears.

Alessio's face lit up and he scurried over to him. I had lost him.

I joined the girls dancing gracefully under the crossfire of the boys throwing carnival confetti and blowing serpentine paper streamers at the chandelier. Mini pizzas were trampled, Fanta was spilled and confetti were pulped into papier-mâché against Mamma's parquet. But I still held hopes of swinging to the music with my sultan.

At one point, when some of the boys began rolling on the floor and getting tangled in the paper streamers, Mamma shrilled:

"Time for a game! Sit in a circle, we'll play spin-the-bottle!"

I couldn't believe my luck! I had played it before and I knew that, if the bottle pointed to me and Alessio, we would have to kiss. It wouldn't have taken more than a gentle blow to steer the plastic bottle that Grandma had pulled out of the rubbish bag and wiped with a napkin, but at that moment I wished for telekinetic powers.

Mamma struggled to persuade the princesses and the fairies to sit on the food-splatted floor, but eventually she managed to and explained:

"If the neck of the bottle points to you, you must hop on one leg for ten seconds."

Hop? What about kissing? Things seemed to be taking a turn for the better when one of the princesses was found cheating, hiding two legs under her puffy skirt instead of hopping. The penalty would have to be changed, I thought hopefully.

And it was changed, but only to "reciting a tongue twister". I lost all interest in the game, until the plastic bottle, too light for the job, after some overenthusiastic spinning, flew out the window, causing a commotion. At that point, Mamma decided it was time for the birthday cake.

I was ushered to the place of honor at the top of the table and made to stand on a chair, high above everyone else—which was nice. When everyone sang '*Tanti auguri a te*', I sang louder than the others and blew out the candles with exaggerated zeal, all the time checking that Alessio was paying me the attention I was due. Unfortunately, he was busy catching up on the pizzette and the arancine.

Then the doorbell rang and parents started streaming through the door. Mamma's face regained color, Grandma disappeared into the kitchen and I realized, to my horror, that my birthday party was almost over. When Mrs. Filigrino came to collect the sultan of my heart, all hopes of spending quality time with my beloved fizzed away. The next time I'd see him, we would be in class and the most intimate exchange I could hope for would be asking to borrow a pencil.

But miracles do happen. As they were leaving and I felt tears pricking my eyes, out in the cool silence of the elevator lobby, Mrs. Filigrino smiled a lovely smile and said:

"Thank you, Marta, for inviting Alessio to your party. Alessio, say thank you to Marta and give her a kiss."

Before I knew it, Alessio's soft lips pressed the sweetest little kiss on my cheek. Then he said "thank you" and disappeared with his mother—that wonderful lady—into the elevator.

I don't remember any of the other presents I received that day—not even what was in Alessio's parcel—except for that kiss.

***

The memory of that birthday party came galloping back to me last Saturday, when I found myself in the unfortunate position of the harassed mother of a birthday girl. Having moved her to a new school, I felt that I could no longer deny Valentina a full-class birthday party and the chance to cement new friendships through it.

While I was laying out the arancine, cursing whoever decided that crumbly, sticky rice balls should be considered party food, my mother's reminder that "at least, this party isn't going to have Carnival confetti and blow-out streamers like yours" didn't boost my morale.

But Valentina's fluttery excitement did, and it also made me wonder if she might have a sweet spot for one of her classmates. Maybe it was just me projecting the memories of my own childhood onto her, I thought. But as the days passed, I became more and more convinced that it must be true, and I prepared a playlist of slow romantic songs.

Finally, on Saturday at 5 p.m., our little guests were dropped off at our apartment by their mothers. Names were pronounced, hands shaken and courtesies exchanged but, after the first few, all the children's names became scrambled together in my brain. We played a rumbustious round of musical chairs followed by an unconvincing one of musical statues' and a dramatic attempt at limbo. When I turned on my romantic playlist and announced the slow dancing, boys and girls drifted to opposite sides of the room like a diffusion experiment played backwards. And Valentina's smile waned. I remembered Alessio Filigrino and my own party.

"Time for a game of 'spin-the-bottle'!" I declared, armed with a full bottle of Fanta. "The penalty will be a kiss on the cheek."

A grin kicked up at the corners of Valentina's mouth.

The first time I managed to get the bottle to land on Valentina, I looked at her meaningfully, hoping for a sign that would help me steer the bottle in her desired direction. But she was staring at the bottle so intently that she didn't notice. I did my best to spin the bottle towards a blond cherub that, I was sure, must be the class heartthrob.

Valentina's facial expression when the bottle landed on him told me I had made the wrong assumption. She obliged, her classmates giggled and clapped, some girls looked disappointed and the bottle spun on. I could tell from Valentina's eyes that she was praying for it to land on someone, but who?

I could only give her one more chance without breaking the illusion that the bottle was spinning at random. After a few more goes that landed on other children, I managed to spin it on her again. This time, she looked intently into my eyes and, arms akimbo, she clumsily pointed a finger in the direction of a boy with a sweet face and lovely brown eyes framed by the longest eyelashes. Of course! He looked just like my old flame.

I closed my eyes and concentrated as hard as I could on spinning the bottle on this boy. A strategically positioned skirt hem (mine) helped ensure that I didn't overshoot. And the bottle landed on the boy.

Valentina leapt up, smiling so much that her cheeks looked like they might pop out of her face and, heedless of the cheering attention of the rest of the class, she rushed to lay a kiss on one of the boy's rotund cheeks. No doubts that I had got the right one. That smile didn't fade from her face until the intercom rang and I announced: "Tommaso, get ready, because your dad is coming up to collect you."

Then he stood up and I learned that Tommaso was his name. Valentina and I accompanied him to the door, following the floor counter on top of the elevator with our eyes. I remembered my anguish when Alessio left the party and felt for my daughter.

When the elevator pinged and the doors opened, a man stepped out. He had the same cheeks, the same eyelashes, the same eyes as Tommaso. He looked at me, hesitating.

"I'm Tommaso *Filigrino*'s Dad," he said, stressing the surname.

My heart leapt as I saw the five-year-old boy in the forty-year-old man. "Alessio!"

"Marta."

I offered him my hand, but he pulled me into a kiss.

3. SOMETHING FOR SUPPER

The service was over and the weekday Mass regulars were chatting across the pews. Anna's daughter had got engaged, excitement was running high and there was still much to talk about when Father Pino ushered them out of the church to lock it up for the night, so the women continued discussing engagement rings and wedding plans on the sidewalk outside the church.

At one point, Melina noticed the darkening sky and remembered that Tanino was waiting for her at home. Her husband didn't like her being out after dark and he knew that Mass ended at six-thirty and that it took her ten minutes—fifteen if stopping at the bakery—to get home. He was probably already worrying.

"I'm sorry, but I have to go now or Tanino will send a search and rescue party for me," she said jokingly to the others.

"My husband was like that too," Peppina said, "but I soon made him lose the habit."

Melina wondered how she'd managed that, but she was too proud to ask. Instead, she brushed off the comment: "Tanino is like that because he loves me."

"Stay, Melina. If he's worried, he'll ring you," Anna

suggested kindly.

"I haven't got a phone," Melina admitted.

"*Really?* You're the only person I know who hasn't got one," Peppina said maliciously.

"I don't want one: it would only make Tanino check on me every five minutes."

Peppina lifted one eyebrow. "That's because he loves you, darling," she mocked.

That irked Melina quite a bit, so she huffily bade them all goodbye. Under a pink and purple sky, she plodded towards her home with her heart in turmoil. Her friends must still be chatting about wedding dresses and parties while was scurrying home like a dog obeying its master's whistle. If the streets were really that dangerous after dark, weren't they also dangerous for her friends, for all the other people treading the pavement around her, and those who worked in the shops, which were open till eight? Tanino was overprotective. Or was he just worried that she wouldn't be able to cook his supper on time? Why didn't he ever cook, take her out, or buy takeout? Melina saw the illuminated plastic cornucopia of the bakery in the distance and remembered that she needed to buy the bread for their supper. Seditious voices swirled in her head, urging her to rise up and revolt. She stopped in her tracks, turned around and walked in the opposite direction, towards the pizza shop.

Sometimes, when Tanino had fancied pizza, she had bought it from that shop. Tonight she wouldn't cook—she was already late for supper anyway—but she'd take home some ready-made pizza. Never mind that the shop was out of her way and that it would take her longer to get home: it was all part of her rebellion and it would teach Tanino to stop breathing down her neck like she was thirteen instead of seventy-three.

Just as she was about to step into the pizzeria, another smell—stronger and meatier—cut across that of freshly baked pizza: roast chicken. It came from the *rosticceria* next door. With sparkling eyes, Melina admired the chickens suspended on the rotating spits, spinning on themselves and around the flames like planets orbiting the sun. She would have happily swallowed the lot like a cosmic black hole but Tanino preferred pizza and that was why she had never been in the shop next door. Still, if there was a time to try out the roast chicken, it was certainly tonight—the night of her rebellion. She whipped around and, instead of the pizzeria, she stepped into the rosticceria, where she ordered a roast chicken and fried potatoes for two. All the way home, a swoon-worthy smell emanated from the parcel and made her mouth water and her stomach grumble.

***

Tanino grumbled to himself: it was dark and Melina hadn't yet come home. He had expected her home at six-forty-five and now the clock had gone past seven. Why didn't his stubborn wife get a phone? He could have called her and put his heart at rest that she was fine.

Maybe she wasn't fine. Tanino imagined her lying on the pavement with a sprained ankle or knocked over by one of the many Palermo bag-snatchers. Or maybe she had only stopped at their daughter's. He rang the apartment downstairs and Rosanna answered.

"No, I haven't seen Mamma today. She must have met a friend along the way. Don't worry, Dad, she'll be home soon."

But Tanino worried: Melina was never late to cook his supper. He had to go and look for her. He searched for his phone, found it at the bottom of a drawer and tried to turn it on but it didn't come to life: the battery was flat. He put it back in the bottom of the drawer—he'd charge it later—took the house keys and set off.

He knew exactly which way Melina walked to church and back, including the precise spots where she crossed the road, which were different on the way there and on the way back. If she was walking home, he would certainly meet her. He reached the bakery. Whenever he wasn't working inside, the baker stood at the entrance by the fly curtain like a decorative lion statue and greeted all his habitual customers as they walked past.

"Have you seen my wife tonight?" Tanino asked him.

"I saw her going to church."

"Not on her way back?"

"No."

Tanino felt himself blanch.

"But, around that time, I'm usually serving inside so she might well have walked past and I didn't see her."

"So she didn't come in to buy bread?"

"No."

Tanino's heart plunged to his feet. "Maybe I should call the police."

"I wouldn't yet, if I were you. Women don't like that sort of thing and you end up playing the part of the jealous husband. She might have got a lift home and didn't feel like asking the driver to stop for bread." He ran an idle finger between the beads of the fly curtain.

"If she had taken a lift, she would have got home earlier, not later!"

"My advice is to go home and wait a little longer. The police won't even consider her case if she's been missing for only half an hour."

Tanino thanked him anyway and set off to the church. At least Father Pino must be able to tell him if she even made it to Mass. A snapped umbrella lay on the ground next to a garbage can. Tanino imagined Melina clobbering a robber with her umbrella—even if the umbrella on the ground wasn't hers.

Father Pino was about to sit down to his dinner but he graciously let Tanino in and answered his questions: yes, Melina had been to Mass, like every evening—he added, unprompted—and had left the church when he had locked up, at around six-forty. Tanino calculated that, even if she had set off home at six-forty instead of six-thirty, she should have been home by seven-fifteen when he left the house to search for her. He thanked Father Pino, asked him to pray for her tonight and, with a heavy heart, plodded home.

***

Melina was very disappointed when she got home and didn't find Tanino. Not least because the chicken was getting cold. Wasn't supper late enough already? What was he doing, gallivanting outside? Maybe he had gone to have his dinner at the *trattoria* down the road. In that case, she should unceremoniously tear open the packet with the chicken and eat the whole lot! But then the thought that Tanino might have gone looking for her flashed through her mind and she stopped. That was a totally unnecessary complication, bound to delay her supper: because yes, in the circumstances, she didn't feel that she should start without him.

Reluctantly, she put down the chicken and picked up the phone. Thank goodness he had a mobile phone. She dialed his number and a recorded message announced that the recipient was unavailable. She put the handset forcefully down on the table before picking it up again and dialing her daughter's number.

"Dad was looking for you, Mamma. If he's not at home, he must have gone out searching for you."

"That's very silly. I wish he hadn't done that. Where has he gone?"

"I don't know but please, don't go looking for him, or you'll miss each other again."

"Alright."

Melina sat on the sofa, clasped her hands, and stared at the chicken. *It won't be too long*, she told the chicken, or maybe herself. But soon her legs were twitching and the smell of the chicken was unbearable. If she stayed in the apartment any longer, she would eat not only her half, but Tanino's too. She got up, grabbed her handbag and set off looking for her husband.

***

By the time Tanino approached their building, all the shops were shut and the streets looked unwelcoming, spooky and dark. At least they seemed so to him, but probably not to the gaggle of girls from the apartment upstairs who filed out of the elevator all dolled up after filling the inside with perfume. It was a strange perfume: it had a base note that reminded him of... roast chicken, of all things!

Funnily enough, the roast chicken smell was still there when he got to his floor's landing, and even inside his apartment. And there was the chicken, wrapped up and sitting on the table! Melina must have bought it on her way home, so that was why she was late!

"Thank goodness you're back, I've been so worried about you!" he called out, looking for his wife in every room.

But the apartment responded with silence.

***

Melina had retraced her steps back to the church. If Tanino was looking for her, he would be doing just the same and she would meet him somewhere along the way. But she didn't.

Now that the shops were shut, she couldn't even ask the baker if he'd seen him. She checked at the trattoria, but he wasn't there—anyway, by this point she doubted that he would be having dinner out on his own. She checked at his brother's house, but he hadn't seen him either. Having run out of possibilities, she headed home, planning to ring the police and report him missing. It was eight-thirty when she thrust her key into the door. *Grazie a Dio* it was unlocked! Her heart levitated in her chest. Tanino must be home!

Sure enough, there he was, sitting sad and bedraggled, staring at the parcel on the table.

"Thank goodness you're back! I've been so worried about you!" she cried. He turned slowly and gave her a wild look.

The chicken was cold and dry, but neither of them complained. After supper, like every night, they sat on the sofa in front of the TV. But, unlike other nights, Tanino lay his hand on Melina's knee, as if to reassure himself that she was there, safe and sound. And she lay her hand on his.

4. SWIMMING IN SINGAPORE

Merilyn watched a magnolia leaf as it was tossed towards the edges of the pool by ripples in the water and thought about her husband. He was a sailor on a huge container ship and the last time she had spoken to him, he had been calling to say that they had just passed a pirate-infested area but were safe.

"Merilyn, look at me," Jake, her employer's seven-year-old boy shouted excitedly from the other side of the condominium's bean-shaped pool, before diving headfirst into the water.

Merilyn's mind raced back to her home in the Philippines, where her own son was growing up with his grandparents. Had he learned to swim yet?

"Merilyn, did you see me?" Jake asked, bobbing out of the water.

"Yes, darling, I did. What a clever boy you are."

A big smile stretched across Jake's face and soothed Merilyn's pangs of nostalgia. She should be happy that she'd found employment with this nice family. She should stop feeling sad.

Wendy, their neighbors' maid, appeared at the end of the path, pulling an overloaded trolley through the manicured garden towards the elevator lobby. Wendy hadn't been as lucky as her. Her employers were mean, never gave her a day off and rationed her food so tightly that the poor girl was losing weight. Merilyn waved at her and she waved back. Tonight she'd try and sneak some fried rice to Wendy through the kitchen window.

"I've had enough of swimming. My skin is burning," Elodie said, leaping out of the water. Jake's older sister was not as easy as her brother. Merilyn had immediately gelled with Jake but Elodie... she was never rude to her, but she kept her distance. If neither of her parents could see her, she'd swim and frolic in the water with her brother, but if Ma'am or Sir appeared on the poolside, she'd leap out of the water and sulk on a sun lounger.

Sure enough, Ma'am had just arrived. She kicked off her flip-flops and untied her sarong to swim. "Oh, don't go now, darling. I've only just arrived."

"My skin is on fire. I'll get skin cancer before I'm eighteen." Elodie wrapped herself in her towel and shuffled towards the block's elevator lobby, where Wendy was already waiting for the elevator. Merilyn watched them standing next to each other, two girls of a similar age, both wet, one with sweat, the other with pool water. Both looking miserable.

***

"Merilyn, could you come here a moment?" Ma'am asked, stepping into the kitchen, where Merilyn was cooking dinner. Merilyn didn't like being interrupted in the middle of a stir-fry—the rice would clump together and Jake wouldn't like it—but Ma'am's tone suggested that there might be a problem. *Oh please, don't let her have discovered that I sneaked food to Wendy!* She turned off the flames which were leaping around the wok and followed her employer with a knot of fear in the pit of her stomach.

"Did you say that you cleaned the curtains yesterday?" Ma'am pinched the hem of the curtains in the master bedroom between her forefinger and thumb.

"Yes, Ma'am, I washed them yesterday."

"But look. They're covered in dust."

Merilyn stepped closer. Yes, the curtain was caked with an ash-like dust. Even on those days when the wind blew the smoke of the Indonesian forest fires across to Singapore, that much dust couldn't settle in such a short time.

"I swear, Ma'am, I washed them yesterday. Maybe someone had a barbeque?"

Ma'am gave her a sidelong glance. In their luxury condominium, the flats were so close that you could see the gold tap of your neighbor's bathroom when you were sitting on your toilet. The condominium's management would never allow a barbeque that smoky. Just then, the doorbell rang and Ma'am went to the door.

"Oh, hello Wendy, how are you?" Ma'am voice drifted in from the hall.

Oh no, it was Wendy, surely looking for her! The poor girl never got enough money for the shopping, as her employer expected her to haggle at the market. But Wendy was too shy for the aggressive haggling that her meagre budget required, so she often ended up returning home without some crucial ingredient. To avoid being scolded, she usually turned to Merilyn who would 'lend' her an egg or some rice or whatever the girl needed for that night's meal. *Not today, please, not today*. Merilyn flung herself down the corridor.

"I'm well, thank you, Ma'am." Wendy's eyes glistened with gratitude. Wendy's employer wasn't the kind who would ask a maid how she was. Merilyn felt a pang of jealousy as she saw Wendy look adoringly at Ma'am and, suddenly, a terrible thought flashed across her mind. The window of Ma'am's bedroom was close enough to the windows of Wendy's apartment. It would be easy enough for Wendy to shake, let's say, the ash of her employer's joss sticks onto Ma'am curtains.

Why would she do such a thing? To get Merilyn fired

and replace her. Merilyn shook her head as if to shake that horrid thought out of it. No, surely Wendy would never do that.

"May I speak to Merilyn for a moment, Ma'am?" Wendy mumbled.

Merilyn's blood froze. Wendy had never been so bold as to visit her when Ma'am Louise was at home. Was she trying to get her into trouble? No, she was probably just particularly desperate today and couldn't wait.

Once Ma'am had left them together, Wendy asked her for a cup of cooking oil and Merilyn gave it to her as usual. But for the rest of the evening, she couldn't help wondering if Wendy was a friend or an enemy.

***

"I love Singapore, Mum, but I'm a little concerned about something," Louise told her mother over the phone.

"What's is it, darling?"

"Some strange things have been happening and I don't know if it's been Merilyn or… The curtains, for example. Merilyn said she washed them yesterday, but today they're like dust sheets. The other day Mike found his magazine all curled up as if it had fallen into a bucket of water. I asked Merilyn about it but she didn't have any explanation. I checked for toppled glasses of water, dripping aircon, open windows, leaky ceiling… nothing. Then, this morning, as I wriggled into my swimsuit, it ripped all along the side stitching. Before you ask, I haven't put on any weight. When I looked for another swimsuit, I found the drawer empty. And the swimming goggles' strap snapped as soon as I put them on. You tell me if all these things can be happening by chance."

"The humidity of the tropics and the heat can play havoc with paper, fabric and rubber straps…"

"Yes, they could, but the magazine looked like it had been dunked into a bucket of water. Mike swears he didn't even touch it with wet hands. And what about the missing swimsuits? I fear that Merilyn might not be quite as good as she seems. If Merilyn hasn't stolen my swimmers, lied about the curtains and maybe dropped water on the magazine by mistake, I can't think of any other explanation than bad feng shui. Our Chinese neighbors warned us that this apartment was bad luck. Elodie's asthma has got worse since we came here."

"I don't believe in feng shui and luck, darling. Don't jump to conclusions. Elodie's asthma could well have got worse with the different air and all the stress—"

"Stress?"

"Sure. The poor girl has had to say goodbye to her friends, her home, her school, her rabbit... By the way, tell her that he's doing very well, he's keeping my lawn nice and short and we've become very good friends. What I need now is a bigger garden!"

***

Merilyn pulled up the blinds and swept around Elodie's bed. The kids were at school, Sir was at the office and Ma'am was working in the English tuition center. All alone in the apartment, Merilyn could let her mind wander back to her home. Last night, her heart had squeezed hard when Aaron squinted into the phone and asked, "When are you coming back?"

Out of compassion, or perhaps just cowardice, she had told him, "Soon".

As she thrust the broom under Elodie's bed, some rolled-up paper tissues tumbled out. She fished under the bed with the broom again and a few more came out. Merilyn knew this sign very well, because she too used many tissues in the night. Elodie must have been crying. There was hardly anything a family could hide from the maid who did their laundry, cleaned their rooms and stocked up their fridges. But in her many years working with different families, Merilyn had learned that it was best for a maid to pretend she didn't have eyes. Once, when she was working for another family, she had noticed that the teen son had started wetting the bed just before his Olevels. When she had mentioned it to the Mamma, hoping that she would stop pressuring him to study harder, she was scolded. She was so glad that her new employers were much nicer.

Oh dear, her luck wasn't going to last very long if things like dusty curtains and sodden magazines kept happening. An unpleasant thought flashed across her mind: Wendy could have splashed water on Sir's magazine through the bedroom window. Tying a cup to a long stick, it would be possible to pour water through the open window. No, it was ridiculous, and she should feel ashamed of even imagining it. But the question remained: how did the curtains get dusty and how did the magazine get soaked?

She was still tossing these thoughts around in her mind when Ma'am burst into the room. Elodie's scrunched-up tissues were still huddled up between Merilyn's feet and the broom. If she wanted to tell Ma'am that Elodie cried herself to sleep, this was the perfect time. Mustering all her courage, she opened her mouth to speak—but Ma'am spoke first.

"Do you know anything about this?" she said icily, thrusting forward her briefcase. Merilyn peered inside. Ma'am's teaching books were all wavy, as if they'd been dunked into the swimming pool, left there for a day and finally left out to dry in the sun. "How wet is your mop when you clean my bedroom?"

"Ma'am, I swear, I always lift your bag from the floor before I mop!"

"Merilyn, I just don't know what to think," Ma'am said, and left the room.

Merilyn felt tears brimming in her eyes. She liked Ma'am and she always did her best to please her—she hated Ma'am thinking badly of her. She felt sorry for Ma'am as she imagined her pulling the books out of her bag in front of her students and finding them all curled, with the pages stuck together. It was beginning to seem like, just like Merilyn was trying not to suspect Wendy, so Ma'am was trying to find an explanation for these strange events that didn't involve her. Merilyn had to help her.

***

Having missed the chance to tell Ma'am about the tissues, Merilyn resolved to take the matter in her own hands and talk to Elodie. As soon as the girl was home from school, Merilyn grabbed a pile of ironing and floated into the girl's room.

"Are you still in touch with your friends back home?"

Elodie's eyes swiveled from the phone's screen to Merilyn. "Yup."

"Do you miss them?"

Elodie pinned her with her eyes. It was a *how-did-you-know?* look.

"I miss mine too," Merilyn went on, "and I miss my boy, my husband, my parents. I know that, at your age, friends matter more than family, but at least you have your family with you, and perhaps you can make the best of what you have. Talk to your parents about how you feel." Merilyn left her words hanging in the hot humid air and left the room before she became unwelcome.

The following day, there were no tissues under Elodie's bed. They were hiding in the bottom of the bathroom's garbage can. Ma'am had no idea that her daughter was crying every night. Merilyn had to tell her, even if her intrusion was the last drop that cost her the job.

***

"You come from Lobo, don't you, Merilyn," Sir asked her as she brought the dinner to the table.

"Yes, Sir."

"Next week I'm going to Lobo for work. Would you like me to take a parcel for your family? I could leave it in the hotel reception and they could pick it up."

"Oh, yes, please!"

Just then, the doorbell rang. *Hay naku*, just when she was about to ask Sir how big a parcel he could take. It was bound to be Wendy, that annoying girl! She scuttled to the door and wrenched it open. Sure enough, it was Wendy.

Merilyn revved herself up to give her friend an earful about disturbing the family's meal and getting her into trouble—she might even confront her about the dust, the sodden magazine and the soaked books—when her gaze fell on Wendy's right cheek. It was round like a curry puff. "What happened to your cheek?"

"Toothache," she muttered. "Have you got paracetamol?"

"You need to see a dentist."

"My Ma'am says it's too expensive."

"She should have medical insurance for you."

"She hasn't got it."

Merilyn's blood boiled. Wendy's employer was breaking the law in so many ways and was blatantly taking advantage of Wendy's fear of reporting her. Her anger was roaring in her head so loudly that she didn't hear her Ma'am approach.

"You need to go to a dentist right now. I'm taking you," she said sternly, grabbing the car keys from the console. "Merilyn, please, look after the rest of the dinner, will you?"

"Sure, Ma'am."

Merilyn watched as Ma'am and Wendy disappeared into the elevator together. Biting back tears of jealousy and fear for her job and future, she closed the door.

***

When dinner was all cleared away and the dishes were done, Merilyn set up the ironing board and started ironing. She usually left that job for the evening because the air was cooler then and because she found it relaxing. Right now, she needed all the relaxation she could get. At nine o'clock, Ma'am finally came home.

"The dentist managed to save the tooth but he was shocked that Wendy had waited that long before seeing him," she reported. Then, looking at the ironing board,

"You don't iron swimsuits, do you?"

"Of course not, Ma'am," Merilyn replied, a little offended.

"Of course. I was only asking because my green swimming suit fell apart as I put it on this morning, and I can't work out why."

Oh, no, not another of the mysterious crimes! "Maybe it was ants?"

Just then, Elodie walked past them with her bedtime chamomile. "Elodie, darling, have you taken my red and blue bikini, by any chance?" her mother asked.

"No, Mum. It's the heat that destroys the elastic," Elodie said casually, walking away.

"Excuse me, what did you just say?"

Elodie turned around: "It's the tropical heat that destroys the elastic."

Ma'am and Merilyn looked at each other, then Ma'am said: "I asked you if you had taken my missing red and blue bikini but you've just told me why my green swimming suit fell apart. I never told you about the green swimming suit."

Elodie's cheeks flamed.

"Elodie, do you also happen to know how Dad's magazine and my books became soggy?"

Elodie's eyes were pinned to the floor. "The humidity in the air did that."

"And, let me guess: the polluted Singapore air covered the curtains in dust, am I right?" her mother pressed on.

As Elodie nodded, Merilyn felt a wave of relief wash over her. It had been Elodie! Now not only was she cleared of Ma'am suspicions, but Elodie's sorrows were about to come out in the open.

Merilyn discreetly pushed the ironing board into the kitchen, closed the door and left mother and daughter alone to talk in the sitting room.

***

"You won't believe it, Mum! It was nothing to do with

feng shui, bad luck or poor Merilyn. It was all Elodie's doing! She was trying to make me believe that the Singapore air was too humid, too polluted and too hot for us to stay here. She misses her friends very much. She really wants to go back to England."

There was a pause at the other end of the line. "Tell me something, dear. Who's looking after your maid's child?"

"His grandparents." Louise thought for a moment, then her heart soared. "Mum, are you saying that…" It was a fantastic idea. Elodie would love to go back to England and live with her granny. It wouldn't be for long, anyway: Mike's overseas posting was only for two years.

"There isn't much point in Elodie coming to live with me…" her mum said, and Louise's heart dropped out of the sky. No, she had misunderstood: her mother wasn't offering it. "…because her school and friends aren't here. Plus, there's not enough grass for her rabbit in my little garden. But Elodie and I could stay in your home together until you all come back from Singapore. Then she could go to her old school and see her friends again. Her rabbit would love being back in his patch, and I quite fancy a change of scene: new parish, new exercise classes… Do they still run the salsa classes near your home?"

"Yes, they do! Oh, Mum, this is the best idea ever! I'm sure Elodie would love it."

***

Merilyn sat on the beach, looking out at the sea. She thought of the people who had changed her life, Ma'am and Sir, far across the waters, in Singapore. Sir had helped her and her husband get a job in the naval engineering factory that his company had just opened. Now they earned enough to live comfortably here in the Philippines and didn't need to work overseas anymore. Soon Aaron would finally get a brother or a sister.

Ma'am sent her pictures of Elodie, who was very happy in England with her grandma, and Jake, who was growing big and strong.

Wendy, too, was growing big and strong. Ma'am had reported her employer, who had been fined and banned from hiring foreign domestic helpers ever again. Wendy now worked for Ma'am and, although she had put on quite a lot of weight, she still looked slender and pretty.

"Look at me, Mommy," Aaron called from an overhanging spur of rock. As soon as he caught her attention, he leapt into the air and dived in.

"Clever boy," Merilyn called out, and remembered the day when she had wished that her boy could learn to swim.

5. A SLIP OF THE TONGUE

Joanna felt like screaming too. Her three-month-old baby was emptying his lungs and his wailing was mingling with the screech of the violin next door. Since moving to Singapore, noise had been a constant background. Train noise, car noise, construction noise, drilling-upstairs noise, pneumatic-drill-in-the-road noise and tropical-rain-lashing-at-the-windows noise.

The sound waves that really rubbed her nerves the wrong way were those from her neighbor's violin. She had once met the likely culprit: a little Chinese girl with ponytails, six or seven years old, dainty as a doll and polite as a Singapore Airline hostess. They once met in the elevator, the girl saddled with a huge backpack, a lunch bag and a violin case. A few minutes after each had got into her apartment, the violin had started screeching and the baby had woken up, foiling Joanna's efforts at getting him to nap. The following time, Joanna had taken the baby out in the stroller to help him fall asleep. Armed with a good book, she had hoped to read and rest on a park bench while the baby slept, away from the violin screeches.

By the time the baby had fallen asleep in the blinding sunshine, Joanna was so hot and tired that she would have happily slept on the bench instead of reading the book, if only she could find anywhere to sit that wasn't scorched by the sun. When she had tried sitting down on a park bench, her legs had felt like sausages on a griddle. She had lumbered to a coffee shop, with her pram too big to maneuver between the tables, and ordered a strong chamomile.

When the school holidays begun, Joanna could no longer bank on violin-free mornings. The scales, etudes and exercises started at eight o'clock sharp, were interrupted at lunchtime and resumed one hour later, to last—with short and unpredictable intervals—until 10 p.m.

"Of all the flats in Singapore, we've chosen to live next to the next Vanessa-Mae," Joanna moaned to her husband one day.

"All Chinese children work hard at their musical instruments. You're just suffering from culture shock," Mark replied, always defensive when Joanna made negative remarks about anything connected with his job posting.

Her mother's suggestion was a little more helpful: "Talk to your neighbors and see if you can agree to a 'protected baby nap time'."

So one afternoon, when the screeching was getting on her nerves more than usual, Joanna picked up her screaming baby and walked across the landing to the next-door apartment. She rung the bell and an elderly Chinese lady opened the door. She stared at Joanna with the frightened eyes of someone who knows that conversation is going to be difficult.

"I'm sorry to ask you, but could you please put off the violin practice until after, let's say, four o'clock? You see, my baby and I need a nap now," Joanna said.

The old lady smiled nervously and muttered something in Chinese in an apologetic tone—possibly that she didn't know English.

Unfortunately, Joanna didn't know Chinese either. "Don't worry, thank you, sorry," she said, resigning herself to another scorching walk in the afternoon sun.

That evening, when Mark got home, he found her lying on the couch with the baby on her chest, both asleep at six in the evening.

"Are you all right?"

"Not really," she said, and told him about her attempts to communicate with their neighbors.

"Ah. You should have used my electronic translator," he said in that irritating way men have of trying to find simple solutions to complex problems.

Joanna wasn't in the mood for anything but sympathy and a back rub. "What makes you think that the old lady can read?"

"The machine speaks, darling."

That night the baby was colicky and restless. Joanna slept little and, when the *koel* bird sang, she was already awake. The morning passed in a semiconscious blur of exhaustion (Joanna's) and wailing (the baby's). When the violin sprang to life straight after lunch, Joanna gave in and searched for her husband's electronic translator. He had left it out on the chest of drawers. She turned on the device and typed frantically:

Please stop this horrid noise, my baby and I need to sleep. We can't sleep with this screeching.

A string of Chinese characters appeared on the liquid-crystal screen. Translator in hand, she hitched her screaming baby on her hip and flew out of her apartment to knock on her neighbor's door. This time, the violin stopped. Both the little girl, violin and bow in her hands, and the old lady appeared at the door, smiling nervously.

Joanna pressed a button and Mandarin sounds poured out of the clever machine. Expecting the smiles on her neighbors' faces to turn upside down, she was surprised when they didn't.

"*Xiè xie, xiè xie*! Thank you, thank you!" they said, beaming toothless smiles at Joanna and at the baby.

Joanna was even more surprised when, as soon as she

had got back to her apartment, the violin started again. What kind of mean joke was this? The only thing that had changed was the tune. Instead of the usual scales and exercises, it was Brahms' lullaby. This time the notes were slow, clear and clean. If there was a mistake, the music carried on without repeating. It almost sounded as if the little girl was playing for an audience. They could try to sleep with that. Joanna lay on her bed with her baby on her chest and they both fell asleep.

***

Mei Ling had hoped for bigger and better things when she had graduated from drama school. But bigger and better things came once a year and the rice bowl needed filling every day, so she had accepted small advertising jobs and voice recordings for books, talking toys and—today—for an electronic translator.

Inside the recording studio, the furry microphone hung before her like a limp rat. She dreamed of being in a famous radio studio, being interviewed about her part in the latest blockbuster. Another day. Maybe another life.

"Again! Keep the same intonation for all the words," the recording manager, a Western man, barked at her.

How could she possibly use the same intonation when Chinese is a tonal language? It wasn't her place to explain this to her boss, especially if she wanted to keep the job. She ignored his request and carried on, hoping somebody else would tell him that it was impossible to do what he asked.

"No, no. You are changing it again. Carry on with the same intonation. I want it to sound happy, like when you said '*mǎ*', I liked that one."

Mei Ling looked at the assistant manager, a Chinese man, pleading for help. He looked away, stone-faced. The sound technician, also Chinese, didn't lift his eyes from the table. Mei Ling mustered up her gumption and said,

"I'm sorry, but '*mǎ*' and '*mǎ*' mean different things."

The boss looked puzzled. "I don't care, it doesn't

sound good once it's recorded. Keep the pitch high and happy and we won't have to stay in this room until midnight."

The windowless, foam-clad room felt claustrophobic. Mei Ling had no wish to spend a second more than necessary there. "All right. Happy and high all the way."

And she did. And because the words were totally different now that she'd changed their tones, she started changing the vowels and consonants too.

***

That morning, Mark took his translator into the office. He was expecting a customer from China and wanted to impress him with some polite exchanges in Mandarin. He turned on the machine and saw Mandarin characters. Joanna must have used it in the end. He pressed the button that made the machine speak but the sentence was well beyond his knowledge of the language, so he walked to one of his local colleagues.

"Jimmy, can you tell me what's it saying?"

He played it aloud, and Jim said:

"It says, '*Please continue this marvelous music. My baby and I need to sleep. We can't sleep without this music*'."

6. SUMMER LOVING

Anna scans my dress, nods and smiles. "You're good to go, darling."

Music wafts from the church's open doors. "What if he's not there?" I say, smoothing down my dress nervously.

"Don't be silly. Of course he's there," she replies, just like she did ten years ago. But this time she adds, "He's right by the altar, waiting for you."

***

It had taken me three weeks to choose what to wear for the end-of-year class trip to the beach. The whole class was going, including Enrico, and he meant everything to me. Each time he turned his jade-green eyes to me, I got lost in their depth, mesmerized by the glittering specks of turquoise, the long blond eyelashes. His hair shimmered golden in the sun and his sinewy body exuded energy. If you had asked seventeen-year-old me to express a wish, there would have been only one answer: being Enrico's girlfriend.

Anna and I had been discussing what I'd wear for the trip to the beach at every breaktime and lunchtime and on every bus journey home. Eventually, she chose not just my swimwear, but also my beach towel, sandals, shorts and T-shirt.

"You look perfect," she said when I picked her up on my Vespa, the day of the trip.

At full speed, we rode down the tree-lined avenue that joins Palermo to Mondello beach. The warm summer air rushed into our shorts, tickling our legs, as the sun warmed our skin and the sea shimmered cheerfully before us, glittery and turquoise. Anna sat behind me like a guardian angel, with her arms around my waist. Every now and she squeezed me in a reassuring hug. As we drove through a patch of ailanthus and eucalyptus trees, a cooler wind enveloped us as their canopies closed over us like a tunnel, dappling the sun.

"What if he's not there?" I asked Anna.

"Don't be silly. Of course he'll be there."

We emerged into the full sunshine. The white beach stretched out before us like an embrace. Our classmates were already there and our eyes scanned the group anxiously.

"He's here," Anna whispered. So he was, as gorgeous as ever. She squeezed my hand. We stretched our towels next to the others on the warm, soft sand and wriggled out of our shorts and T-shirts as gracefully as we could, like butterflies emerging from their chrysalises.

Those of us who spent our weekends poring over textbooks slathered our shoulders and the tips of our noses with sunscreen, while we admired and envied the others' tans. The boys kicked off their flip-flops and pulled their T-shirts off their backs by the scruff of the neck, the way boys do, while darting furtive glances at the girls. Not much was left to the imagination once we were all down to our swimmers.

Enrico's body gleamed in the sunshine like Michelangelo's David. Next to him, the other boys looked like earlier drafts. Carlo kicked some sand at Anna and me, shouting, "Last one in the water is a nincompoop!" but didn't sprint to the water immediately, as if waiting to see if we would follow. Meanwhile, Enrico leapt to the challenge with long bouncing strides and easily beat Carlo to the water.

"Last one in the water is dry and warm!" one of the girls shouted back. She wore a white swimming suit. She would regret it the moment it got wet. Others ran to the water. It was the best place to hide your body if you felt self-conscious. Carlo jumped in too, shouting, "Come in, the water's not too cold!" at Anna and me.

"Alright, but no splashing," Anna warned, as one of the other boys was getting ready to do just that. We held each other's hands, Anna and I, as we sank our feet into the warm sand, and I thought that soon I'd be enveloped by the same water where Enrico was swimming.

"Don't be pathetic. Jump in!" Enrico shouted at us, emerging from the water like a sea god, dripping droplets that sparkled in the sunshine. He flicked his long wet fringe off his eyes with a clean sweep of his neck. He looked like Adonis, Poseidon and Cupid all at once.

Then his gaze locked into mine and a mischievous grin curled his lips. "Maybe you need a little help." He set off up the beach with long leaping strides, bounding straight towards us. He was going to pick us up and launch us into the water, but surely he couldn't pick up both at once. What if he chose Anna? The thought alone wrung my heart. "Don't you dare!" I shouted at him, my voice dripping with challenge. He veered neatly towards me. My heart soared. He grabbed me behind my knees and swept me off my feet, holding me tight against his chest, which was still cold from the sea water. I made a lame show of protesting while my heart soared into my neck with the excitement and pleasure of feeling his thumping heart against my side.

"Don't you dare drop me!" I piped, wrapping my arms around his neck. It was pure bliss.

"I won't," he said, and he didn't. He kept holding onto

me as he walked further and further into the sea until we were completely submerged. The excitement and the shock of the cold water took my breath away, which was all the better as we were underwater. We smiled at each other in the crystalline sea, wrapped in a blissful, bubbling silence. In those precious moments, I found myself wishing I was a mermaid—or any other creature that could stay underwater forever.

Instead, I had to bob up, gasping for air. Dizzy with exhilaration, I glanced back to the shore, checking for Anna, and saw her smile. I also saw Carlo swimming towards us. I didn't want him to join us. "Let's swim to the pontoon," I told Enrico. He flew off swimming, butterfly style, his shoulders opening like the wings of an angel as he weaved through the water. The pontoon was crowded with younger kids, but Enrico heaved himself up and made himself space. When I finally reached him, he made space for me too, and one of the children next to him fell into the water. Sitting next to each other, hands resting on the pontoon, almost touching, I had it all. I asked him how he'd learned to swim so well, and he told me that he was in a swimming squad and a lifeguard. He also told me that he was a member of the regional volleyball team and dabbled in archery too.

I hadn't had time to tell him about my hobbies and he hadn't asked yet, when Carlo reached us, panting with the effort of the swim. Neither of us made space for him, but he didn't take the hint to leave us alone. So I said, "Let's swim back to the shore."

Enrico dived headfirst, elegant as a dolphin, and I followed him.

Back on the shore, the others were playing volleyball. Enrico leapt out of the water and titled his head to me as an invitation to join the game. I hated volleyball but I smiled and nodded. If Enrico had asked me, I would have walked into a blazing fire.

But then I saw something that changed everything.

Three children were building an impressive sandcastle, complete with mote, bridges and turrets. Its only architectural fault was that it lay between us and the volleyball match.

"Watch out!" I called to Enrico, but it was too late. He walked straight into it, treading on bridges, turrets and walls. The smallest of the three children burst into a desperate wail. Enrico shrugged and walked off.

In that instant, he fell out of my heart like a lump of lead. How could such a beautiful creature be so uncaring? His jade-green eyes, his golden shimmering hair, his perfect body had tricked me. Perhaps choices about love were best not made in summer.

By the time I reached the crying child, Enrico had already barged into the volleyball match. His making space for me on the pontoon no longer seemed like an act of gallant courtesy, but an expression of insensitive arrogance. His swimming off ahead of the others was vanity and one-upmanship, not admirable physical prowess. "I'm sorry about your castle," I said to the children. "Can I help you rebuild it?"

"Yes, please. Can we make it bigger?"

"Sure. Bigger and better." *Like people's hearts should be.*

"Would you like a hand?" Carlo asked behind me.

He was still panting from the long swim.

I turned and looked up at him. His eyes weren't the color of the sea, but the color of the earth, from which flowers grow. "Yes, please."

It was only when somebody sent the ball into the water that Enrico noticed me helping the children with their sandcastle. He never came back to say sorry.

We called the new sandcastle *Neues Schloss* because it was new and the children had decided that it was in the German Black Forest. When the sun started to plunge behind the sea and everyone packed up to leave, Carlo asked me very quietly and very shakily if I wanted to go for an ice cream with him. I said that I had to check with

Anna because I had given her a ride. When I asked Anna she gave me a big knowing smile and said that she had been offered a ride by Antonio.

I never found out if that was true, but Carlo and I went to the *pasticceria* opposite the beach. Much to our surprise, they had Black Forest cake which, of course, we tried and found delicious.

***

Carlo is by the altar, smiling at me. His warm brown eyes sparkle with tenderness and love. I shudder to think what might have happened if Enrico hadn't stepped on that sandcastle.

The three sandcastle masons, now teenagers, come forward with a box. Our wedding rings dangle from the turrets of a beautiful miniature castle made of glass. I look at Carlo with tears brimming from my eyes. "Glass is just sand, melted together," he says. I nod. So are we.

7. A WOMAN'S WORK

Tanino and Melina had been married for forty-five years and, like in many other Sicilian couples, for all forty-five of them Melina had done all the domestic chores. That morning was no exception.

While Melina washed up the breakfast's *caffettiera* pot, Tanino stared longingly out at the kitchen balcony. "I wonder where Rosanna is now."

It was the first time that their daughter and her family were going on holiday without them. It wasn't that they hadn't been invited, but Tanino and Melina had never been on an airplane and they didn't fancy starting now.

"She should be landing," Melina replied.

"Only landing? It feels like they've been gone for ages!" Tanino sighed.

"Let your daughter have some peace with her family," Melina retorted, a little jealously.

"We're her family too," he observed sadly. A blaring ambulance siren filled the silence between them. "What if we fall ill while she's away?"

"If you fall ill, I'll look after you. If I fall ill, you'll look after me," Melina said curtly, holding little faith in the second part: not only was she rarely ill, but when she had been, Rosanna had stepped in to help, as she only lived in the apartment below theirs.

As Tanino stared at the airplanes' vapor trails, Melina was overcome by a prickly, unpleasant mixture of resentment, irritation and feeling put-upon. Why had she always looked after Tanino but he had never looked after her? Why was he exonerated from housework, even now that he had retired from work? That was when she hatched her little plan.

***

"I'm not feeling well. I must have caught that flu everyone is talking about."

"Flu? In August?" Tanino sat up in bed and gave her a puzzled look.

"Yes. I saw it on TV: it comes from Australia, where it's winter now. It travels on airplanes." Melina gave a little burst of a cough to confirm her diagnosis.

"But you haven't been on an airplane."

"Yes, but Peppina has, and I had coffee with her two days ago."

Tanino jumped out of bed as if the invisible flu virus was soaking through their shared sheets.

"Have you checked your temperature?"

"Of course not: I've been in bed. As you're up, can you get me the thermometer? But before anything, I need my coffee."

"Where do you keep the pot?"

It turned out that Tanino didn't know where Melina kept the coffee, the sugar, the coffee cups or the thermometer: he had always asked Melina when he needed anything. It took quite a few instructions shouted from her bed before Melina finally received her coffee.

While her husband was in the bathroom, she dipped the tip of the thermometer into her coffee and pulled it out when it had reached the desired temperature. "39.1°C!" she announced.

Tanino shot out of the bathroom and stared

incredulously at the thermometer. He was about to check Melina's forehead with his hand, but suddenly retracted it, thinking better of any physical contact with her. Panic glazed his eyes.

"What are we going to do?"

"Me, I'm doing nothing: I'm sick."

"I'll call the doctor!"

"*No!* I mean, no. They say on TV that this flu goes away in four to five days, if you rest in bed." Melina could see the cogs in Tanino's brain working: five days was too long to eat takeout pizza, too long to leave the dirty laundry to pile up, and too long to leave the floor unswept.

"I'll be very weak for some time after that, but I should be out of bed in five days," she added.

Tanino clapped his hands together and shook them in despair. "What a rotten piece of luck! Just when we're all on our own!"

***

When he realized his predicament, Tanino felt a chill go down his back. How was he going to look after his sick wife and himself, when he had never touched the stove, the oven or the washing machine? On those rare occasions when he had timidly tried to make himself a coffee, Melina had stormed into the kitchen and told him off for using the wrong *caffettiera* pot or the wrong burner. He felt an irresistible urge to run away and come back when Melina was well again, but that was not an option, especially now that Rosanna was away.

So, going back and forth between Melina's bedside for instructions and the rest of the house, he attempted—and managed—to put on a wash, hang the washing out to dry, cook pasta with tomato sauce for lunch, and do the dishes. When he had finished all this, it was already time to prepare for dinner. Then, after more dishes, he took the dry laundry in, folded it and put it away. By bedtime, he was exhausted.

While on the first day every task had taken him forever,

on the second day he was much quicker and, as he fancied pasta with tuna, he went to the fishmonger, bought the tuna, and cooked it following the fishmonger's instructions. He grinned at the surprise etched on Melina's face when he served it. Supper was a simple salad with leftover tuna cooked in the grill-pan. As he sprinkled an oil and lemon dressing over the plates, he felt like one of the chefs on TV. That night, when he went to bed, he was tired but also really pleased with himself: not only had he found out that he could cope, but he had also enjoyed the power of deciding what to eat. And, lo and behold, he loved cooking!

The only cloud hanging over that day had been Melina's increasingly irritable mood: the woman really didn't take well to being bedridden! If he accidentally let a pot slip and made a little noise, she would shriek from her bed, demanding to know what was going on. At one point she even appeared on the kitchen threshold in her nightgown. By then, he had started to suspect that her sickness had been a masqueraded, but he was happy to play along with it.

"It doesn't matter that you don't have a fever anymore. If yesterday you had a temperature of thirty-nine, you still need to rest to avoid a relapse."

***

On the third day of her 'sickness', Melina got out of bed before six o'clock. She couldn't bear to spend one minute longer in that damn bed—three days had been long enough, thank you very much.

Also, imagining what Tanino might have done, loose in *her* kitchen for three days, gave her more goose bumps than any fever, imaginary or real. When she gingerly opened the kitchen door, much to her surprise—and, to be strictly honest, disappointment—she found all the counters tidy, a pristine floor, and a fridge well-stocked with groceries that she had not bought. The discovery was more unsettling than if she had found another family sitting down and eating in her kitchen. Her little plan had backfired: she had lost control over her little world.

She pulled out a chair and sat down on the balcony for a little fresh air and thought of Tanino's grin when he served her his pasta with tuna. How could Tanino have changed like this? Looking back, she remembered times, early in their marriage, when he had made timid attempts to make himself useful in the house. Back then, she was too young and proud to let him. Maybe he had always wanted to be more involved in the domestic chores. She had been silly—she felt it keenly—and resolved that, from that day on, she would share the kitchen and the chores with Tanino.

An early morning flight streaked the sky with its vapor trail. Rosanna would be coming back soon. She wouldn't believe the power of a bout of summer flu.

8. LUNCH ON ST LUCY'S DAY

Twenty-four-year-old Francesca Liotta was determined to prove herself an impeccable wife to her newlywed husband, Girolamo Grassi.

Three months into their marriage, she decided that it was time to meet his colleagues and show them their new home. She would treat them to a home-cooked lunch that would increase Girolamo's standing in his workplace—the bishop of Palermo's Curia, where he worked as an accountant. Being very confident in his wife's culinary abilities, Girolamo much approved of the idea and together they set the date for Saturday the 13th of December.

They sent out the invitations, bought extra chairs for the table, and planned a menu which catered for Reverend Ingotta's intolerance to dairy, Rosa and Marina's vegetarianism and Father Pasquale and Father Giuseppe's madness for fish.

After weeks of deliberation, they came up with the perfect menu: tomato and basil bruschetta as a starter, linguine with truffles as a first course, grilled fish with vegetarian sausages as a second course and dairy-free lemon sponge with lemon sorbet on the side as a dessert.

A few days before the event, Francesca stocked up on the fresh ingredients, took the dustsheets off the sofa and the chairs in the living room, opened the expandable dining table and pulled the embroidered organza tablecloth that had been a part of her dowry out of the chest of drawers. The wedding flutes came out of the glass cabinet, the silverware went on the table and the gold-rimmed plates were dusted and laid out on the twelve places. Twelve places for twelve apostles, she thought, with amusement.

Everything was laid out and ready, expect the food. A frisson of fear ran down her back as she wondered if her cooking would be up to the occasion. That night, she slept a dreamful and restless sleep.

The next morning, she got up early, cut the vegetables, prepared the fish, and laid out each pot and pan on the stovetop, in its special place. She would start the cooking half an hour before the guests arrived, but now she needed to buy the bread: for, according to any Sicilian, a hunk of bread that's more than a few hours old is only good for breadcrumbs.

At 10:55 a.m. Francesca picked up her purse and trip-trapped down the stairs to the baker's to catch the eleven o'clock batch of freshly baked bread. But...

...it was shut. She couldn't believe it: except for two weeks in August and Sunday afternoons, her baker never shut. She rattled the metal shutters to check if it was a joke. No: it was really shut. Maybe the owner had had a sudden bereavement. Francesca made the sign of the cross and scurried off to the baker's down the road.

That was shut too. It was Saturday morning, wasn't it? What was happening? Wild-eyed, she ran to the baker's in the main street. That one must be open: it had two bakers who worked day and day on rotation, making bread in the day and croissants in the night for the hungry youth back from the nightclubs. Shut.

Francesca was now quivering with frustration. A

middle-aged lady who was passing by, stopped. "The bakers' are closed, darling: it's the feast of Saint Lucy."

Francesca slapped her forehead. Suddenly, it all made sense. Palermo people didn't eat bread on St. Lucy's day since, in 1646, during a terrible famine, a ship laden with wheat grain had landed in the port on the saint's day and saved the inhabitants from starvation. The people were so hungry that they didn't wait to mill the grains but cooked them whole and, from that day on, on the 13th of December, the devout in Palermo didn't eat pasta, bread or any milled wheat.

The consequences hit Francesca like a full-speed train: of her entire menu, only the fish, which Girolamo was going to simply grill in a pan, was appropriate to entertain a group of priests and Catholic workers on that day.

"But I'm sure that some of the bakers in the town center will be open for the tourists," the other woman suggested helpfully.

Francesca managed to utter a 'thank you' before walking away with a knot in her throat. Creating a vegetarian, dairy-free and wheat-free menu in the half an hour she had left before the guests started arriving was impossible. Even if she turned the linguine with truffles into a risotto with truffles, there was no time to cook a risotto now. In fact, looking for a bakery that was open, she had wasted so much time that she hardly had time to get herself dressed and put on her make-up. She wished that the pavement would crack open and swallow her forever.

Then a delicious smell wafted into her nostrils. It was coming from a café, where crispy breaded rice balls were sitting next to chickpea-flour fritters and other deep-fried treats. It seemed that everyone had remembered the feast day except her. She should go in and buy the stuff. No, what a failure of a wife would she be if she served takeout to her husband's guests?

But a fasting lunch wasn't an option. It wasn't even

Lent. Francesca hesitated outside the door for a few seconds, watching people pouring into the shop and out of it with big steaming parcels. The arancini rice balls started disappearing from the window. People were buying large quantities. If she wanted those arancini, Francesca had to act fast. She whipped into the shop and was just in time to secure the last ten: five vegetarian and five meat ones. She also bought the *panelle* chickpea fritters and a few other bits and pieces that the serving girl recommended, or that looked simply too delicious to miss.

With her steaming hot parcel and a heart still unsure if she had done the right thing, she plodded back home.

"Where have you been, darling, I was getting worried!" Girolamo exclaimed when she opened the door of their apartment. Horror of horrors, the guests were already there and she was meeting these people for the first time in her slacks, without make-up, holding parcels of take-away food. Her cheeks burst into flames. As they brushed cheeks for the customary air-kisses, she was sure that the guests were being burnt.

Once they were alone in the kitchen, Girolamo approached her. "What happened, darling?"

"It's St. Lucy's day."

"Oh, dear, we had forgotten. Well done for buying this food—"

"Hello! I've brought some *cuccìa* I've made with my grandma's recipe. It's fantastic, you have to try it," Marina said, stepping into the kitchen with a large bowl of the traditional porridge pudding for St Lucy's day.

"Great. Now we have everything, including dessert!" Girolamo said cheerfully.

But Francesca was fighting back tears. None of the food for that meal had been cooked by her, while the guests had brought home-cooked food. She was a complete failure.

During the meal, Girolamo squeezed her hand under the table. "It's going very well, don't worry," he whispered into her ears. But neither his tender looks not the guests' cheerful conversation could get rid of that horrible feeling that she had let him down.

When they were tucking into Marina's dessert, Rosa asked her abruptly: "What's your maiden name, Francesca?"

Francesca had noticed Rosa glancing furtively at her all through the meal and had become convinced her that she hadn't managed to repress her tears convincingly enough.

"Liotta."

"Ah, I knew that I had seen you before! You're my daughter's teacher! I'm Giulia Leone's mamma."

Francesca went as rigid as stale bread. Now her shame—the wife who can't cook—would spread to her workplace too.

"Giulia can't stop telling me how wonderful you are. All the kids love you. It seems that you've turned even the tone-deaf ones into musicians."

"Me?"

"The children absolutely love you and all the parents were raving about your end-of-year concert."

"I'm delighted to hear that." Francesca could sense Girolamo's chest filling up as well as her own shoulders lifting.

"I've heard that you restore your own instruments, is that true?" Rosa continued excitedly.

"Yes. I have restored the harpsichord that's in the sitting room."

"You must play it for us!" demanded Reverend Ingotta.

"Yes, you must!" the others joined in.

"With pleasure." She smiled.

When they'd finished their dessert, Francesca made everyone a coffee and sat at the harpsichord. As her fingers flitted across the keyboard and the plucked strings vibrated with music, everyone listened, spellbound. Father Pasquale was caught blowing his nose and wiping shining eyes when Francesca had finished playing and everyone congratulated her for the music, for the beautifully refurbished instrument and for the coffee which, apparently, tasted delicious. A squabble ensued between Reverend Ingotta and Father Giuseppe, as one wanted her to play at the Bishop's Christmas concert and the other wanted her for the Carmelites' Convent centenary, which were on the same evening. Francesca looked at Girolamo and saw him beaming with pride. Then she beamed too.

9. A CRAFTSMAN'S ART

"This is an almighty mess, I'm not having anything to do with it!" burst out Domenico, tossing the pliers onto the marble floor. The others glanced at Adriana, their boss.
"It's good enough. The conference is on Monday," she retorted.
"Adriana, it's the wrong alloy and it shows. This is like repairing a jewel by replacing diamonds with bottle bottoms."
"You're just getting hung up on subtleties."
Subtleties. A 'subtlety' that would make them infamous for centuries to come. The restoration 'experts' who destroyed the eighteenth-century meridian line.
The brass line glinted across the cathedral's nave and aisles. Generations of men and women had turned to it to synchronize the heartbeat of their town—clocks, railways, feast days—with that of other towns across the continent. And not just that. The meridian was also a piece of art, born out of the meeting of the Enlightened Sciences and the Arts. Inlaid marble zodiac signs flanked the brass rail, so skillfully intricate that you'd be forgiven for imagining marble to be as soft as clay. The meridian certainly demanded more respect than a hasty patch-up with

bottom-standard brass.

Adriana would not have been acting this way if it hadn't been for the damn astronomy conference. It would have been much better to admit what had happened—that the funeral contractors had stabbed the soft brass rail with their cheap coffin frame and gouged out a section— rather than repairing it badly and hoping nobody would notice. Of course people would notice. The astronomers, for a start. They weren't coming all this way, from all over the world, to give the meridian a passing glace. They certainly wanted to see it in action. Sunlight would shine through the gnomonic hole up in the vault, down onto the meridian line at midday, in a different place according to the day and the season.

But Adriana had said—in her 'I've-been-told-by-people-high-up' voice—that the incident with the funeral contractors wasn't good for the city's image and must not be divulged. Everybody knew who those 'people high-up' with whom she rubbed shoulders—and other parts of the body, too—were. So they had all kept quiet, including Domenico.

Only the year before, when a wasp nest had covered the gnomonic hole, Adriana had deemed it too risky to entrust the clearing of the nest to a pest control contractor, so they had dealt with it themselves. They had even used a paintbrush to remove the debris and matched the paint for a touch-up. How could she now pay so little attention to the very line which gave purpose and reason to that hole?

She had left for lunch. It was her usual way of dealing with dissent.

A beam of sunlight, piercing the damp darkness of the nave, rushed to kiss the meridian's glistening rail. It must be almost midday. Dust particles, as if awoken from a centenarian slumber, danced in the energizing beam of light. The same light that caressed the creamy stone outside felt like a laser cauterizing Domenico's bruised heart.

That night he dreamed of stepping up on stage to receive a prize but, instead, rocks and metal scraps were being hurled at him by an enraged crowd which was shouting: "He destroyed the line!"

He woke up panting, drenched in sweat, his heart rattling his ribcage. Images of the wounded meridian whisked around in his brain. Negligence of this magnitude would destroy his professional reputation. It'd be the end of his career. All those years at the Academy of Fine Arts for nothing.

Panicking, he decided that he must have nothing to do with the meridian, even if it meant resigning. He got up, fired up his computer and began ferociously typing a resignation letter. He was fast asleep at 9:15, when the phone rang.

"Domenico, where are you? Please, don't you be sick too. Carla and Giuseppe have already called in sick. We can't manage without you. Come as soon as you can. By the way, your brass sample has arrived," Adriana said over the phone.

Giuseppe and Carla were never sick. What were the chances of them being sick together? Surely they were trying to wash their hands of the meridian. Never mind: the brass sample had arrived so there was still a chance of repairing it properly. He flung the resignation letter into the wastebasket, jumped into his work clothes and rushed to the car.

"Finally! Your brass sample is on your desk," Adriana chirped when he arrived.

In an exhilarated frenzy, Domenico tore open the packet, pulled out the piece, rushed it to the meridian and compared them, holding his breath. Color... shade... sheen... texture... a perfect match! The sick patient had found a donor. He turned to the crucifix on the altar and whispered *'thank you'*, even if he hadn't thought of himself as a believer in a long time.

Then he cut, filed, heated, bent and hammered the metal

into shape. A few hours later, wrapped in a clean cotton cloth, he marched it to the sanctuary and laid it down next to the meridian. The transplant organ was ready and pulsating.

Ever so gently, he coaxed the piece into the hole. It was supposed to slip in like a hand into a glove. It didn't. What slipped was Domenico's hand, clutching a set of pliers, which crashed onto the tip of Taurus's horn and made it crumble.

Horrid profanities echoed in the empty cathedral, punctuated by the sound of Domenico's furious footsteps striding out. He burst out into the square, flung chisel and pliers against the gravel and cursed some more.

It took a few cigarettes and Gianni's comforting pats on the shoulders before Domenico returned inside to inspect the damage. The Taurus looked silly and sorry without the tip of its horn. Replacing just the tip was out of the question. Bulls' horns have no joint. He would replace the whole horn with the same brown marble from the same quarry. Nothing less would do.

After the first round of phone calls, it emerged that the quarry had been shut for decades. A second round of enquiries produced somebody who knew of somebody who was aware of the existence of a certain derelict building containing a decorative basin possibly made with marble from that quarry.

The next day, Domenico spoke to a man who said he was the owner of the building. He'd sell him the sink for 'only' one thousand euros, because they were 'friends'.

After a quick stop at the ATM machine, Domenico drove out of town and reached a deserted dirt track which would have made a perfect set for a Mafia film. Out of the pocket of his jeans went the cash and into the Fiat Punto went a beautiful basin, bearing the signs of having been hastily hacked from its original location. No receipt. Anyway, he'd never be able to claim this money from work.

Puffing and panting, with Gianni's help and a trolley

borrowed from the baker, Domenico unloaded the basin from the car and plonked it onto his workstation.

He inspected it from all angles, shining a torch across from all directions, before choosing a section with the right grain and veining, which he broke off with chisel and hammer. A shame about the beautifully carved acanthus leaves, but that was life. Then he modelled the piece into a crescent shape, flat on one side, and carried on carving, chiseling, and polishing until a horn identical to the original one emerged.

Domenico would have carried on polishing and perfecting into the night, if Giuseppe hadn't forced him to go home. That night, he couldn't sleep. The next day, his hands were shaking so much from all the espressos and the lack of sleep that Adriana entrusted the task of replacing the taurine horn to Giuseppe and Carla—who had both mysteriously recovered.

While Carla's tapering fingers tickled the hurt horn out of its ancient alcove, Domenico paced the nave like an impatient father-to-be. Giuseppe brushed off the debris and gently slipped in the new horn. It fitted like the crystal slipper on Cinderella's foot. Domenico's heavy sigh echoed through the cathedral vault.

"Are you happy now?" Adriana said in a condescending tone, then to everyone, "Now I want all your desks and cupboards tidied and cleaned. Tomorrow TV crews will shine their cameras everywhere so everything must be in tip-top shape."

***

It was the first time Antonio had seen the city's rooftops from the cathedral roof. Normally it was the other way around: he'd admired the magnificent yellow stone building from just about every direction in all the years he had repaired roofs all over town. It still amazed him how people in the past had managed to build a huge thing like this without bulldozers and cranes. He wondered how many fingers, limbs and lives had been lost to a slipped stone or the lack of harnesses.

The sky was glowing pink. He never worked so late in the day—the light wasn't good at this time—but the walkway could only be fixed when it was closed to the public. Down in the car park, three shiny coaches were swallowing their loads of pale-skinned tourists. Tomorrow more would come and the walkway had to be fixed and dry before then.

Antonio picked up his trowel and swirled the mortar in the bucket. It was just right; it was time. He never hurried his work: no point in doing a job badly. He checked each of the eighty-four metal feet which held the platforms. He filled the gaps where the metal had come loose and wiped off the excess mortar with extra care. This was no ordinary roof, it was the city's cathedral, he kept reminding himself.

Half an hour later, Antonio had finished and sat down for one last glimpse of the cherry-pink stripes across the sky. He'd probably never get a chance like this again. The tower bell struck seven. Time to go home. He picked up his stuff and gave one last glance around. Hold on...

There was a hole in one of the domes! Big enough for one finger, maybe two. Could it be for electricity cables? But there were no cables anywhere near it. He squatted close, prodded the hole with his fingers and peeped in. He could see the glinting brass of that strange line that sliced the nave's floor in half. *Caspita*, so the hole went all the way through! How could anyone leave a hole like that in the cathedral roof? No wonder there were problems with damp!

Luckily, he had a spit of mortar left in his bucket. That should be enough. He scooped it up with the trowel, slapped it into the hole and carefully wiped off the excess with the trowel. All done. Antonio congratulated himself and set off home.

10. ALL THE WAY FROM AMERICA

"Do you know what he looks like?" the sailor asked Giuseppe.

Giuseppe's mouth was too dry to speak. With shaking hands, he reached into the pocket of his duffel coat and pulled out a sepia photograph, worn at the edges and faded in places, of an African American GI.

"Of course! What a stupid question," said the sailor. "Did he say he would be coming?"

Giuseppe nodded. No word could get through the knot in his throat.

The wind whipped foamy crests on the surface of the sea, even inside the harbor. It felt sharper and smelled different from the sea air back home in Sicily. It smelled of ocean.

The gangway was empty; all the other passengers had gone. Giuseppe thought of Grandma and Grandpa's house, the fig tree with leaves bigger than people's faces and fruits sweeter than the sugar cube he got at Christmas. Grandpa, who boasted that he could bring old shoes back to life like Our Lord had brought Lazarus back from the dead. He hadn't been able to do that with Mamma. And there was Grandma, who could mend anything, including people. She hadn't been able to mend Mamma, though. The tubercu-something, whatever its name was, had been too strong for her. But Grandma and Grandpa could have taken care of him, if he had stayed there. Perhaps coming to New York hadn't been such a good idea.

"Do you have his address?" asked the sailor, scanning around.

Giuseppe nodded and the movement shook a tear off his cheek. The sailor was from Sicily too, and Grandma had paid him some money to look after Giuseppe on the journey. But it hadn't been a lot of money—Grandma didn't have a lot of money—and Giuseppe saw him shuffling his feet and tapping impatiently when his mates came down the gangway all dressed for the town.

"Meet you there later," the sailor shouted at them. Later when, Giuseppe thought? What if his father never came?

***

Every time a letter with an American stamp had arrived, Francesca had torn it—unopened—into four pieces and had thrown them into the fire in winter and into the sea in summer.

She ignored the villagers gossiping about her, muttering "*moglie e buoi dei paesi tuoi*"—'wife and oxen from your own country'—or when they called Giuseppe 'the mulatto child'. The simple reason was, she had fallen in love and married a black soldier from America. Apart from her parents, nobody from the village, not even her relatives, had said as much as 'congratulations'. Her parents were brave and rebellious like her, but maybe it would have been better if they had opposed the marriage, like everyone else.

When the Americans arrived in their trucks, showering the village children with sweets and chewing gums, and sharing their cigarettes with the grown-ups, the people cheered them like they were angels sent from Heaven. The air was redolent with the scent of the blossoming weaver's broom, the day their trucks filled the mountain roads. She was collecting prickly pear pads to make cutlets for supper when their trucks thundered past her along the dirt track. The soldiers were singing and they looked well-fed, healthy and happy. They didn't look like they ate cacti stems for meat.

One vehicle stopped and the driver got out. Louis was as black as the people from Africa she had seen in picture books. He was tall and muscular, his teeth whiter than the inside of shells and his lips sensuously full. She was using the rusty top of a can to cut the cactus stems and he offered her his penknife, speaking in a voice deep and velvety like she had only ever heard on the radio. She accepted the knife with a blushing smile and a nod.

Then, in broken Italian, he offered her and her prickly pears a ride back to the village. She reckoned that her parents' disapproval of fraternizing with soldiers only applied to German ones, so she accepted.

"My name is Louis," he said.

The enormous truck he drove was his mechanical equivalent: tall, big and with a deep, gravelly voice. His palm felt warm, smooth and dry when he offered her his hand to help her up into the cab. The other soldiers made space for her and they rode along the bumpy track, laughing heartily each time a hole in the road tossed everyone off their seats. She had no idea what any of them were saying. She didn't have an ear for languages, unlike Louis, whose local dialect got better every day. Yes, because after that afternoon, he turned up at her doorstep every day, now with a present of chewing gum, now with a tin of squashed meat, always with a bouquet of wildflowers.

But as soon as the villagers noticed them together, they began to interfere. "Stay away from him. Can't you see he's black?"

"The Three Kings were black too and baby Jesus didn't mind," she replied at first, but then she became fed up and her replies became sharper—"He's no blacker than your heart"—and made her enemies.

They were engaged and married in the military office. A church wedding, with bells and a white dress and children throwing rice and flowers, would come another day, she thought. But it didn't.

Instead, Giuseppe came along. Louis had already gone back to America with the troops. He wasn't there when Giuseppe was baptized, when he took his first steps or when he started playing with the village children. Louis wasn't there to protect him when the other children teased him and taunted him because he was different from them. Louis had promised to come back for his wife and his child once he found work and bought a house for them in America. It would take time, but he would work his knuckles raw to make it happen, he had said.

Six years passed and he hadn't come back for her and Giuseppe. She stopped reading his letters and started putting them in the fire. They were full of lies. She heard stories of foreign wives and fiancées abandoned, the men returning home to their old girlfriends and wives as if nothing had happened. These stories hurt more than village gossip. And there was Giuseppe, asking for his father every day...

***

"Giuseppe, there's something I want to show you," Grandma said the day after his mother's funeral. She took him by the hand and they walked to the geranium patch, at the sunny end of the garden. She bent down, pulled a rusty spoon out of the soil and started digging.

"Is there a treasure?" the boy asked.

"Sort of."

Giuseppe joined in the digging with a flat stone. A dark green glass bottle peeked through the soil. "A pirate's bottle!"

"Not quite."

Grandma lifted the bottle out of its earthy cradle and

broke the wax seal with a knife.

"There's paper inside! Is it a treasure map?"

"In a way. It's a map to find your father, Giuseppe. I salvaged the sender's address from one of his letters before your mother burned it, and I buried it for you. A man who writes to his family every day cannot but love them. Your mother, bless her, didn't think so, but now you can find out the truth by yourself. If you want, we'll find your father."

***

"Giuseppe!" a tall black man shouted, running across the wet pier towards him.

Giuseppe felt his heart leap through his ribcage like a puppy out of its pen. Giuseppe clutched the photo. This man looked like the one in the photo, only without the uniform. He looked more like him than any of the men in the village back home did, and he knew his name, even if he pronounced it in a strange way. "*Papà?*"

"Yes, Giuseppe, I am."

His father grabbed him under the armpits, lifted him up and squeezed him hard, wet cheek to wet cheek. Then he said, in broken Italian, "I am so sorry that your mother... I wanted to have everything perfect for you both—a house, a good job, food on the table—and I worked as hard as I could, believe me, but I waited too long."

Giuseppe looked at this stranger who was his father and wiped the wetness off his cheek. "Don't cry, *Papà*. I'm here now."

His dad looked into his eyes—deeply, searchingly. "You are so much like your mother. She couldn't have left me a better gift than this."

11. A CLASS OF THEIR OWN

"Ladies, I have some news to share," Katie said at the end of our Thursday morning aerobics class.

"Has someone said, 'cake to share'?" Teresa asked from the back row. Everyone laughed, although she probably didn't mean it as a joke.

"You're always thinking about food, Teresa. What am I going to do with you?" Katie replied teasingly. "No, my news is not about cake, although you could say that the two have something in common, as they both stretch your tummy."

Some of us were quick to guess and gasped.

"Yes. I'm expecting a baby," Katie announced, beaming.

The whole of the Thursday morning fifty-plus aerobics class clapped and cheered, a throng of congratulations filled the sports hall and we all huddled around Katie to tell her how pleased we were about her news. This baby had been much awaited and some of us had said a prayer or two for Katie's wish to come true.

"You'll take it easy, now, Katie, won't you?" Maureen said.

"Yes, don't overdo it," Gladys instructed in a stern,

motherly tone.

Even before being born, Katie's baby had already collected a pantheon of honorary grandmothers fussing over it.

"You don't need to demonstrate the exercises anymore, you can just watch us: we know what we're doing now," I told her.

"Thanks. I'm sure you do."

Then an awkward silence fell. Gladys broke it, giving word to what most of us were wondering: "At some point, you'll have to stop doing our classes."

Katie bit her bottom lip and her toned shoulders slumped a little: "I'm afraid I will. I'll have to take some time off, maybe three months, maybe more. But the sports center will find a substitute to keep your classes going until I come back."

"It won't be the same without you," Miranda said.

"But you take however much time you need, Katie," Maureen insisted.

"Yes, don't worry about us, we'll be fine," we all said, even though in a little dark corner of our hearts we *did* want her to think of us and we *didn't* believe that we would be fine without her. After more good wishes for Katie, we finally filed out of the hall and let Katie's next class file in. Gladys' lips twitched as she fought the urge to tell the incoming ladies about Katie's news.

When the pumping beat of the other class started, we were still in the lobby, gathered around the water fountain, some of us filling our bottles, others just unable to leave without talking a little more about Katie's big news.

"Well, isn't that marvelous?" Teresa said. "Next Thursday I'll bring some cupcakes to celebrate!"

"You and your cakes!" we laughed. "We're here exercising to keep in shape and you tempt us with cakes!"

"Alright, I won't bring them next week, but I'll definitely bring them to our last class," Teresa conceded. A palpable grey cloud swept in, dampening our spirits.

"Does anyone know when our last class will be?" I asked.

"We should ask at reception," Miranda suggested.

"When our last class is is not the point," Gladys said pointedly.

"What is, then?" I asked.

"The point is who will be her substitute? That's the crux of the matter."

There was a sharp intake of breath for some, water for others.

"Only Katie knows how far I can push my knee," Julie said.

"She can tell just from glancing at us when it's time to change exercise," Fleur said.

"What if they give us a really young instructor?" Miranda said, wide-eyed with fear.

"Katie is young," I pointed out.

"I hope they don't give us some stick insect that makes us all feel like whales!" Miranda followed on from her train of thought.

"Or a fitness fanatic who drives us into the ground, shouting at us," Teresa said.

"It's an aerobics class for the over-50, not an army bootcamp," I reminded her.

Gladys intervened: "But the matter stays: the new instructor won't know anything about my wrist, Julie's knee, or Teresa's… lazy bottom."

"My bottom isn't lazy: it's just large!" We all laughed, including Teresa.

But we still went home with a heavy heart. We had prayed for this day to come and we were happy for Katie, but we were also sad to see her go, even for a short time. Was it even going to be a short time? Would she come back after having her baby? We had a wonderful rapport with Katie and no change of trainer could be for the better. It was also possibly true that we just didn't like change.

A SLIP OF THE TONGUE

***

The following Thursday morning, as we were waiting outside the hall for our class, Gladys arrived in a hurry, gave us a conspiratorial look and gestured to us to come closer. We gathered around her.

"I have spoken to the powers-that-be," she whispered, "and explained our concerns. They promised me that they'll give us a proper, experienced instructor, not a whippersnapper straight out of training." We all breathed a sigh of relief.

As we went into class, we soon noticed that Katie didn't seem to be her usual lively self. She looked drawn and, unlike the week before, she only did the first of each exercise, sitting out the rest.

"Are you okay, Katie? You look a little pale," Gladys asked her during a short interruption in the music.

"Just a little tired."

"Have you told your doctor?" Maureen asked.

"It's normal to be tired when you're pregnant, isn't it?"

"You might as well tell your doctor, just in case," we said.

"Alright, I will."

***

The following Thursday, we weren't too surprised when the receptionist told us that Katie had started her maternity leave early. A flurry of worried questions hit the poor receptionist. "Is she unwell?" "Is the baby all right?" "What did the doctor say?"

"Both mother and baby are fine, but she needs to rest, the doctor says."

"I suppose our class is cancelled," Gladys said.

"No. Her replacement has kindly agreed to start today."

"Today?" Miranda echoed.

A tense silence descended. Were we going to meet the new instructor just like this, with no preparation?

"Yes, right now. Robert is the hall, ready for you."

"Robert?" Teresa repeated.

Whippersnapper or mature, slim or portly, loud or quiet, one thing was sure: none of us was expecting a man. Just then, as if on cue, the music—Katie's music—started booming from the hall. If we didn't go in, Robert would eventually come out looking for us. We all looked at Gladys. She straightened her back, lifted her chin and led the way into the hall.

***

Our jaws dropped when we saw him, but not in a good way. Robert looked older than the oldest member of our group—either Fleur or Sue, depending on whom you asked.

"This is a joke," Gladys muttered disdainfully. "I asked for an experienced instructor. They didn't have to pull someone out of retirement. I'm sure they could find someone in between a whippersnapper and… Methuselah!"

As a comforting ritual, each of us religiously put down her water bottle and coat in her usual square of floor and we went to stand in exactly the same spot we usually took.

"Welcome, ladies. I'm Robert and I'll be covering for Katie for a little while. Do you have any questions?"

No one spoke.

"Great, then let's begin!" he said energetically.

We started the lesson with the same exercises that Katie started with, and the entire lesson went on exactly like Katie's. It was obvious that she had briefed him and I felt reassured. It was as if Katie's protection was fluttering above us like a spirit.

At the end of the lesson, Gladys shot out of the hall and we all followed her. The entire class was soon gathered by the water fountain.

"Isn't he good-looking?" Teresa said, doe-eyed.

"He's doing the same exercises we do with Katie!" Miranda said.

"That's the point: we are, while he just stands around

and watches us," Gladys said. "He's giving us the same exercises Katie gave us so that he doesn't have to demonstrate them, that's all. If you ask me, at his age, he hasn't got the strength to lift a finger."

"Oh." Suddenly, our eyes were open.

"I was only joking when I said that he's handsome," Teresa clarified.

"This is a practical joke by the management office, and I'm going to protest again," Gladys announced belligerently. A frisson of worry run down our sweaty backs.

***

I had seriously contemplated the possibility of skipping that week's class: if Gladys had gone to complain to the management again, what would their revenge be this time? I didn't want to find out. It appeared that half our class was thinking along the same lines, as I discovered when my curiosity eventually compelled me to go. I arrived early so that I had a little time to mentally prepare for any further changes. I pulled out a chair and sat at the table by reception. I imagined our gentle aerobics class transformed into a full-on Zumba class or a dervish's dance. I was the first one there. The door of the men's changing room opened and Robert come out with a towel around his neck, red-cheeked and wet from the shower. He didn't look like the elderly infirm that Gladys made him up to be, rather like a man tired after a hard workout. He nodded a greeting and I nodded back.

Fleur arrived soon after and, as Gladys's neighbor, I immediately quizzed her. "Any news? Has Gladys complained to the management?"

She gave a little trill of a giggle. "Yes and no. This is what happened." She pulled out a chair for herself and one for me. "To go to the management office, Gladys had to walk through that corridor over there, right?"

"Correct."

"That corridor goes past the weight room, right?"

I nodded.

"She gave a little peep inside, as you can imagine Gladys would, just out of curiosity. You won't believe what she saw." Fleur took a deep breath.

"What did she see?" I almost shouted.

"Robert. Glistening with sweat, muscles bulging under his singlet, weight-lifting belt around his waist. She could hardly recognize him. And you won't believe the weight he was lifting."

"How much?"

"I don't know, but it was a lot. Then he turned towards the door and Gladys had to pretend she hadn't seen him and walked away. By the time she had reached the management office, as you can imagine, Gladys had changed her mind about what she was going to say. She asked about him, his background and training."

"What did they say?"

"He's one of the pioneers of aerobics, trained directly by Jane Fonda." There were gasps from me and the other ladies who had joined us. "And he's a triathlon champion and professional swimmer. At seventy-nine." More gasps and dangling jaws. "It turns out that he doesn't do the exercises with us because, by the time he does our class, he's already run eight kilometers and swum one thousand meters and he has four more classes after ours."

A respectful silence fell around the water fountain as Robert walked past us on his way to the hall for our lesson.

Gladys didn't turn up that day, probably out of embarrassment, but she came to the following lesson, laden with enough cake for everyone, including Robert and the sport center's management.

***

From that day, Robert was accepted and respected by all, revered by some, idolized by others. Teresa was joined by a few more in her admiration for his handsome figure, especially when the summer temperatures forced him to wear shorts instead of long sweatpants.

Katie gave birth to a healthy and chubby little boy and, one day, she came to visit us with her baby. The question on everyone's minds—"Will Katie return?"—was answered.

"I'm sorry, but I've decided to stay at home to look after Jack," she announced nervously. Teresa's sigh of relief was heard loud and clear and everyone laughed. We all wished Katie the best in this new chapter of her life and carried on our aerobics lessons with our beloved Robert.

12. VIEWING RECOMMENDED

Sheila smoothed her skirt and sat down at her new desk. Eight fifty-eight. In two minutes her colleagues would turn the sign to 'open', unlock the glass door and her first day as an estate agent would begin. Who would be her first clients? A couple setting up home together? A growing family in need of more space? It was a privilege to be part of that magical moment when a house is chosen to become a home.

The bell tinkled against the door and a young couple, tightly wrapped in their coats, walked in. The girl sitting near the door directed them to Sheila and, after they had passed, gave Sheila the thumbs up. Sheila felt grateful for the encouragement: after being a stay-at-home mother for twenty years, she had lost some of her confidence in her ability to work outside the home.

A SLIP OF THE TONGUE

"Good morning, I'm Sheila Woods. Please take a seat," she said, struggling to keep her voice steady. She pointed to the two chairs tucked snugly before her desk.

The man pulled his chair away from the other one and sat down. The woman sat on the second chair, collecting her long skirt as if afraid that it might touch the man's leg.

"How may I help you?" Sheila asked cheerfully.

"We need to sell our home," the woman said at the same time as the man said, "We want to sell a property."

"Alright. And are you looking to buy somewhere else?"

"No," they answered in unison.

"How much do you think we can sell a two-bedroom semi on Wisteria Street for?" the man added quickly, as if to steer the conversation back to the house to sell rather than the non-existent one to buy.

"I wouldn't want to say before inspecting the property. Shall we fix an appointment?"

"We are available now," he said.

"Good, I'll come and see it right away. How may I address you?"

"Mr. Jones," the man said.

"Mrs. Jon—actually, call me Linda," the woman said.

The front lawn of 22 Wisteria Street was as uniform and compact as a good-quality carpet. Yellow daffodils and white hyacinths bloomed inside the neatly-edged flower beds and a miniature ornamental cherry stood in the middle of the lawn, making it look bigger. Sheila snapped away with her wide-angle camera. A garden like this couldn't be achieved with some hasty transplanting just before a sale: Mr. and Mrs. Jones must have loved that house. Why were they in such a hurry to sell it?

The hall was tidy but a peculiar duplication of objects—two coat stands, two shoe racks—jarred the eye. In the sitting room, there was a certain asymmetry about the sofa, which was less than pleasing. Was it the fact that the cushions were all piled at one end? Was it that the armchair and the far end of the sofa looked well used, but the part of the sofa in between looked abandoned? Perhaps Mr. and Mrs. Jones had their favorite spots, one on the sofa, the other on the chair. Did they never sit on the sofa together?

"Why you are selling this property?" Sheila asked. It was a perfectly reasonable question for an estate agent to ask, but Sheila had started to fear that the answer might be a private one.

"We are divorcing," Mr. Jones said.

Everything made sense now. She wondered what had gone wrong between them but, of course, she couldn't ask. It was none of her business. But she felt sad for all the hopes, dreams, hearts that had been broken.

She took her photos, made her notes and moved on to the next room. Upstairs she started with the study, which turned out not to be a study after all. Toys, crayons, and picture books were scattered over a pink carpet.

"Oh, so you have a child!" Sheila exclaimed with ill-concealed surprise. She had never seen a home blessed with the presence of children which didn't bear any sign of them anywhere other than in their bedroom. Now that she knew that the young couple had a child, Sheila felt even sadder about their divorce.

"Yes. We've got a three-year-old son. He's staying with his grandparents this weekend. He doesn't know about the house sale yet," the woman said.

"Does… he know about… the divorce?" Sheila asked tentatively and immediately regretted it. It was unprofessional.

"Not yet," the other woman answered. A shadow of pain flitted across her face but she quickly recovered herself and forced a smile.

"Have we finished with this room?" her husband asked sharply.

"Yes, yes," Sheila said, and hastened out of the room.

The master bedroom looked tired and unloved. Two built-in identical closets stood next to each other, one with the doors hanging open, full to bursting, the other half-empty.

"We should we move some stuff from this closet into the other one, so that we can shut the door for the photo," Sheila suggested.

Husband and wife exchanged a glance, then Mrs. Jones puckered her lips and, without a word, pulled some of her clothes out of the overflowing closet and stuffed them under the bed. Not in the other closet. But, even now, the door hung crookedly from its hinges.

"It won't look very good in the photos, with the door askew," Sheila said. "How about you get that fixed and I come back another day to take more photos? You might also like to put a light-colored duvet cover or a bedspread on the bed, maybe even a vase of flowers on the windowsill. You can't imagine what a difference these little things make when it comes to attracting a buyer through our website. You might even want to consider giving this room a new lick of paint."

"Alright."

"How soon would you like me to come back?" Sheila asked.

"As soon as possible," Mr. Jones said.

"I'll call you in the morning as soon as I see a sunny sky. If your back garden is anything as good as your front one, with a bit of sunshine we can take marvelous photos."

Sheila was right. The Joneses' back garden was something special. Flowerbeds burst with pansies, anemones, crocuses and tulips. A lot of work and love must have gone into it.

"Are you sure you want to sell?" Sheila whispered to the other woman.

Mrs. Jones' eyes turned glossy and she hesitated, then glanced to check that her husband was out of earshot and said, "I don't want to sell at all, but I can't afford to buy my husband's half."

The other woman's confidence emboldened Sheila even more. "Whatever it is that has gone wrong between you, can't it be resolved?"

"We started drifting apart when Tilly was born. We'll never go back to how it was before."

"No, you'll never be a young childless couple again, but you can find a new way of being together."

A SLIP OF THE TONGUE

"It's too late," the woman said, gesturing vaguely at their surroundings. Was the house sale the reason that it was too late to salvage her marriage? Deep in her heart, Sheila hoped that the house wouldn't sell. By the time she left the house, Sheila had a plan. Yes, she would lose her commission and perhaps fail her probation and lose her job, but she knew she had to do it.

The following Saturday, Sheila accompanied an elderly couple to 22 Wisteria Street.

"But this property is not at all central," the man said, "and my wife hasn't got a driving license."

"I'm so sorry, there must have been a mess-up with your file," Sheila apologized. "As we are here, would you like to see this property anyway, just as a comparison? Then I'll take you to town."

The couple agreed and they were met by Mr. Jones. He and Sheila learned that the couple had been married for sixty years and had had to leave their country to get married because they were of different religions.

The next viewers were the Browns. 'But... this isn't a bungalow," they said as they lowered their son's electric wheelchair out of the van.

"I'm awfully sorry. I must have entered your details incorrectly in the computer," Sheila answered. But Mr. Jones was already waiting for them at the door so they felt obliged to view the property anyway.

Next was Mrs. Cappello, dressed in black from head to toe and with a locket round her neck. She seemed to like the house very much, until she asked incredulously:

"It's for sale for one hundred and twenty-five thousand pounds, right?"

"Oh no: two hundred and fifty thousand pounds," Mr. Jones corrected her.

"Oh." Mrs. Cappello darted a puzzled glance at Sheila.

"I must have made a mistake when entering it into the computer," she said.

"I'm sorry, but it's totally out of my budget now that my husband has passed away."

Mr. Jones didn't get cross with Sheila for bringing yet another unsuitable buyer, because he was busy fetching a tissue box for Mrs. Cappello. He almost looked like he might need a tissue too.

Weeks went by, the daffodils in the flower beds were replaced by the snapdragons, but no offer had been made on 22 Wisteria Street.

"Any news? How come nobody wants to buy our house?" Mr. Jones asked Sheila every week.

And, each time, she lied, "I'm doing my best, Mr. Jones."

When autumn arrived, Sheila told the Joneses, "The winter months are always very quiet and the garden won't be at its best. How about we take the house off the market and put it back on next spring? Then we'll advertise it as 'new on the market', the garden will be blooming and you're bound to get good money for it."

The Joneses could have complained about Sheila's repeated mistakes, could have asked to be assigned another agent, or could have changed agency. But they didn't.

Instead, they agreed to let the winter pass and said that they would be in touch again in the spring.

All through the winter, Sheila worked hard, selling houses and apartments and keeping her customers and bosses happy with her job. All the while, she prayed and hoped that the Joneses could made things work and save their marriage. Every now and then, when she felt the need for reassurance, she drove past 22 Wisteria Street and checked that there wasn't a 'for sale' sign from another agent. And each time there wasn't.

On a sunny March day, the shop's glass door tinkled and a young couple walked in with a little girl. As Sheila recognized her very first clients, her heart jumped. Where they here to put their home back on the market? *Oh, please make them just be popping in to say hello!*

With her voice trapped in her throat, Sheila gestured to the chairs before her. This time, they sat down without pulling the chairs apart. Was this a good sign? But Mrs. Jones looked pale and pinched, so the divorce must still be on. Sheila offered tea and coffee to the parents and toys to their child. She fussed over the child, talked about the weather, did everything she could to put off the moment when they would instruct her to put their home back on the market. But eventually Mrs. Jones spoke.

"We've come to put our house on the market again…"

Sheila flopped back in her chair in hopeless surrender.

"…because we need a new house," Mr. Jones finished his wife's sentence.

Sheila sat up straight.

"I'm ten weeks pregnant and we need a bigger home when the baby arrives…" Mrs. Jones said, beaming. "Thank you for *all* your help. Truly."

13. A MATTER OF COMMITMENT

An open-top Mercedes C-Class skidded into Villa Lingualarga's car park, sending a flurry of gravel onto the geranium beds. The driver was late and she must have known it, because she squeezed out of the car when it had barely stopped and leapt up the grand staircase without so much as a glance at the villa – or at Don Pericle, waiting for her at the top.

Don Pericle loved to study new clients from his favorite spot, under the budding wisteria, at the top of the baroque staircase: the type of car they drove, who drove and how, whether they waited for each other or not, told him a lot about the bride and groom-to-be. Much of his job as a wedding organizer was about understanding his clients, what they wanted and what they needed. They two were seldom the same, and Don Pericle always felt that it was his duty to deliver the second rather than the first.

On this occasion, what struck him most about his new client was that she had come on her own.

"Hi, I'm looking for the Duke of Lingualarga," she said. She was a beautiful woman, with a bosom that commanded almost as much attention as her piercing blue eyes. Some clever make-up highlighted the mesmerizing power of those shiny sapphires. She was an attractive woman, Don Pericle surmised, who knew that she was beautiful.

Like many others, she had fallen for the duke's trick: both as a test and for a bit of fun, he always welcomed new clients in gardening dungarees and wellies, looking like the estate's gardener. "You're speaking to him. Pleasure to meet you, Signorina Liotta," he said, taking her hand and kissing it.

Her carefully styled eyebrows twitched slightly upwards with surprise at the hand-kissing. "Oh. Nice to meet you. Please, call me Isabella."

"And you can call me Pericle. If you would like to follow me into the study, we can have a little chat and then I'll take you around Villa Lingualarga."

"I look forward to it."

The click-clack of Isabella's kitten heels on the polychrome marble floors and the jingle of her bracelets accompanied their progress through the corridors. As her eyes swept over the frescoes, the stucco putti and gold-framed mirrors, she let out little gasps of admiration which filled Pericle with pride. After his predecessors had squandered the family's wealth at cards, it had been only his hard work and dogged determination that had saved his ancestral home from falling into the hands of developers. He had started the wedding business both because he loved accompanying a couple's first steps into marriage, and because the villa's maintenance was eye-wateringly expensive. The roof of the ballroom now needed repairs and Isabella's wedding was just what was needed to fund it.

"I love this rococo look, Don Pericle."

"The stuccoes are by Francesco Alaimo, doors and mirrors are by Girolamo Carretti."

"And this sculpture! It looks like a Canova…'

"It is: *Pan and Syrinx*, by Canova."

"I'm going to have a wonderful wedding here!"

"I'll do my very best to make it so. And here's my study," he said, opening a door decorated with floral motifs into a room clad in emerald-green damask. Like the wizard of Oz, Don Pericle had his own Emerald City.

Things started to go wrong when Isabella sniffed the air. "Aged leather, a delicious scent. Which brand do you use?"

"I beg your pardon?"

"Don't you use a scent machine?"

"Do you mean those things that some shops use, which send out baking smells even though they're not baking at all?"

"Yes."

"Heaven forbid, no: everything is genuine here."

"My company makes them." Isabella twisted her mouth and tossed back her ebony hair. Then she walked up to the desk in the middle of the room, put down her car keys on the dark green leather writing pad and sat down in one of the two chairs opposite it. Don Pericle went and sat down behind the desk.

"May I ask some information about the groom? When will I have the pleasure of meeting him?"

Meeting both the bride and the groom before their wedding was one of Don Pericle's essential rules. If he wasn't convinced that they were suited to each other and both willing and ready to marry, he wouldn't host the wedding. Sometimes this resulted in cancellations which hurt him financially, but he wouldn't even consider behaving otherwise.

"You can meet him the day of the wedding."

Don Pericle's eyebrows shot up. "I'm sorry, but that's too late. I really need to meet him before."

"Well, that's not possible," she said curtly.

"A video call would suffice." He had never done one, but he would work out how to do it, if need be.

"Impossible." She tossed her hair back.

"Why?"

"Because he doesn't know about this."

Don Pericle straightened in his chair. "He doesn't know that the reception will be here?"

A cheeky smile flashed across her face and she shook her bangles to see her watch. "He doesn't know that he's getting married. Shall we look at the rooms?"

Don Pericle stared at her in amazement. He was sure that he had heard correctly, but how could the groom not know that he was getting married? "Pardon?"

"He doesn't know that he's getting married," she repeated dismissively, as if it was a piece of trivia, not worth delaying her tour of the villa. "The morning of the wedding, I will go to his house at nine o'clock and propose. That leaves us enough time to get ready for an eleven o'clock wedding. The reception will be here, at one."

Don Pericle shook his head as if to shake off his discombobulation. Was Isabella of sound mind? "What if he says no?"

"He won't. We've discussed marriage before. He's just too scared to make the move."

"Scared of what?" Pericle tried to push away the unkind thought that her man might be scared of her.

"Of commitment."

"Then it makes perfect sense that you should propose but… why not organize the wedding only after he says yes?"

She heaved a sigh and shook her head as if Don Pericle was being difficult on purpose. "I know him too well: he'll get cold feet in between."

Don Pericle scratched his beard. Her answers sounded logical and confident, and still he didn't get it, to the point that he was starting to doubt himself. "What about the guests? You asked for a room for fifty people. Are they all in on the…' – the first word that came to his lips was "joke' but he caught himself in time – "…surprise?"

"The guests know that they've been invited to lunch here, but don't know why."

"So, if your fiancé-to-be should say no to the proposal, and the wedding was cancelled, the guests would never know?" Don Pericle hardly believed that he was trying to find a logic in this topsy-turvy, absurd plan.

She sat closer to the edge of her chair. "I can see that you are worried about me cancelling on you. I'll tell you what: for your peace of mind, I'll pay the full fee upfront." Her blue eyes flashed with defiance.

"I can assure you that my financial loss is the least of my worries."

"Then, to answer your question: our guests will know everything, because I will live-stream my proposal on social media."

Don Pericle ran a hand over his face: a public proposal followed by an immediate wedding. The woman was off her rocker! A wave of sympathy for the unaware groom-to-be welled up in his chest: what gargantuan pressure the poor man would have piled on him! Isabella's plan was obviously to leave him no room for escape. There was no way Don Pericle would play along with her scheme. Through the window, he took one last glance at the western wing's collapsing roof and heaved a sigh. "I'm sorry, but I don't agree with this plan. Unless the groom-to-be is fully briefed and I meet him well in advance of the wedding, I can't be a part of this."

Isabella's piercing blue eyes widened, then narrowed, then she grabbed her keys and stood up with an angry jangle of bracelets. "I'm sure that if our genders had been the other way round and the surprise had been for the woman rather than the man, you wouldn't have batted an eyelid. I shouldn't have expected anything better from a stuffy old aristocrat."

Male chauvinism felt to Don Pericle like a most unjust accusation: in forty years as a wedding organizer in a Sicilian village, more than once he had risked life and limb to rescue a coerced bride. But he didn't say a word.

Unsatisfied by his reaction to her bait, Isabella piled it on: "If I'd been afraid of risks, I'd still be mixing fragrances on my kitchen table instead of managing a factory of seventy employees. It's a shame that you're not brave enough, Duke of Lingualarga, because I loved your villa. But I have no time to waste trying to persuade you. There are plenty more handsome villas in Sicily. Farewell."

Cowardice was another unforgivable insult for the duke, but again he didn't rise to the bait. He silently watched as the young woman gave him one last furious look, whipped around and stormed off.

***

"Hello. Am I speaking to Don Pericle?" a woman asked as soon he answered the phone.

He recognized the voice, but he couldn't put a name or a face to it. "Speaking."

"I came to you two years ago, I'm not sure you remember me… Actually, I hope you don't remember… I'm Isabella."

There was a moment of silence, as Don Pericle conjured up his memories. It took some time, as it was often the case with unhappy memories, which he always tried to let go of, while the happy ones he meticulously stored. Yes,

Isabella was the woman who had stormed out of Villa Lingualarga because he wouldn't cooperate in her scheme to trap her boyfriend. But that had not been the end. Realizing that she would find another wedding organizer willing to play along, Don Pericle had considered it his moral duty to contact her boyfriend to warn him. With his niece's help and the help of something called Facebook – whatever that was – he had managed to send a message to the man. If he had received it, Don Pericle never found out, because he didn't receive either a reply from him or an angry message from Isabella. Was she calling him now to give him an earful? Revenge is a plate best served cold, but two years was a long time…

"I remember you. Hello, how are you?" he said warily.

"I'm sorry for how I behaved. I hope you'll forgive me."

So, she wasn't calling for revenge! "It's all in the past, my dear. Don't worry."

"When I left your home I was furious, and even more after you sent that message to Antonio. We argued badly and didn't see each other for a whole year, but it was for the best. You were right when you thought that he would not be pleased about my plan. You saved me from a major embarrassment and from losing Antonio forever. After one year apart and then another year starting from scratch, it's all come together. Last night, Antonio proposed to me. I wasn't expecting it at all, Don Pericle, and I had put no pressure on him whatsoever, whether you can believe it or not. And he gave me the nicest surprise ever."

Don Pericle smiled with pleasure. For a few months after sending that message, he had wondered how Isabella's boyfriend had reacted and if they were still together. Now he knew.

"He thinks the world of you," Isabella continued, "and he's going to ask you to host our wedding. He's right next to me, waiting to speak to you, but first I wanted to say sorry to you, and thank you. We owe you so much."

14. THE STOLEN PISCES

"Thank goodness you're here, Domenico! Somebody has played a nasty joke," Giovanni said, running a hand over his face as Domenico strolled into the workshop.

"I can't take bad news first thing in the morning. Not before my coffee," Domenico replied wearily, but Giovanni shook his head and, pulling on Domenico's arm, led him out the door of their workshop, through the sacristy and into the body of the cathedral, which wasn't yet open to the daily throng of tourists.

Their steps reverberated in the silence as they walked towards the presbytery, where the eighteenth-century brass meridian line slashed the marble floor. That line, which had synchronized the heartbeat of Sicily with the rest of Europe for centuries, glinted proudly in the light that filtered through the stained-glass windows.

"Not the meridian line again…" Domenico still remembered the horrible day when the meridian line had been damaged just before the astronomers' conference.

Giovanni didn't reply but stopped by the zodiac signs of Scorpio and Pisces. Opposite the black marble inlay of a scorpion, two gaping holes stared back at Domenico like startled eyes.

"*Dannazione*, damn it! Where are the *pisces*?" The two marble fish were gone, without a fragment or a speck of dust left to bear witness to their existence. "This is no accident, Giovanni. Somebody has lifted them clean out of the floor. Who would do that?"

"I don't know, but we've got to get them—or some other fish—back in there before the Easter celebrations, or people's shoes will dig into the holes and make the problem worse."

Domenico went back to the workshop, grabbed his helmet and jumped back onto his Vespa just as the delivery boy from the café opposite crossed the road with his espresso. Unfortunately, this morning his coffee would have to wait.

***

The original fish had been carved out of *Albicocca* marble from the Lavigna quarries and Domenico would only be content with the same marble, no less. The road to the quarry wound up a hill for a good fifty kilometers. Domenico's Vespa wheezed up, now faster, now slower, like an old lady lugging bags of shopping up the stairs to her apartment.

When he finally stopped in the dusty car park, the engine felt hot against Domenico's leg. Lorries whizzed around him, lifting clouds of dust, and the sun glared down on the white slabs of cut marble that lay everywhere. At the front desk, a middle-aged lady with half-moon glasses was talking on the phone.

"I'm sorry, but the son is away. You can talk to the father… oh yes, he is the boss. Alright, I'll put you through now." She was startled when she put the phone down and noticed Domenico standing on the other side of the desk. They probably didn't have many visitors, Domenico concluded.

"Oh, good morning, how can I help you?" She pushed her glasses up her nose nervously.

"I need a small piece of your *Albicocca* marble."

"I'm sorry, but we don't extract the *Albicocca* anymore. The vein has run dry."

Domenico's heart sank. "A thirty-by-thirty centimeter slab is all I need," he pleaded.

"We might still have the odd piece knocking about in the warehouse. We can have a look. If we find it, which address should we send it to?"

"I want to take it away now. I can wait."

"You might have to wait a little while—"

"I'll be fine. I can't do any work without it anyway."

"Alright. Help yourself to coffee," she said, pointing to a battered-looking coffee machine in a corner, "and I'll get one of the men on the job."

Domenico thanked her and went to investigate the machine, while the woman left through a back door. The coffee cartridges had run out. Domenico gritted his teeth and tried to distract himself from his need for coffee with the marble samples displayed on shelves. He ran a hand over their polished surfaces and beautiful veining. If he managed to get hold of a piece of *Albicocca* this morning, he might just have enough time to cut it and carve it today, tweak it to perfection tomorrow and have it ready for the solemn Chrism Mass on Thursday, when hundreds of people would be trampling the cathedral's floor.

The back door opened and Domenico jolted. Unfortunately, it wasn't the receptionist, but an old man with small blue eyes and the skin of someone who has spent his life outdoors in the Sicilian sun.

The deep wrinkles around the man's eyes turned into a smile and his blue eyes lit up as he saw Domenico. "Oh, a visitor! Good morning and welcome." He scuttled up to Domenico. "This is *Tramonto Rosa*, our latest production. It's beautiful but also sturdy. A combination you don't easily get—especially in women. We found it last year, by chance. There was a marvelous pink sunset and the men who were excavating didn't realize that the marble was actually pink: they thought it was just the reflection of the sun." The old man unveiled the secrets of each sample with the enthusiasm and passion of somebody who really loved his job, and Domenico listened, spellbound. "This is *Albicocca*, our oldest. We've been extracting it for centuries and it's running out fast."

"Your receptionist is looking for some *Albicocca* marble for me."

"This one, *Pesca*, is almost the same color and has a much more interesting texture. We have plenty and it's much cheaper."

"Unfortunately I need the *Albicocca*. I'm a restorer at the cathedral."

The man's eyes opened wide. "Then you're right: only *Albicocca* will do. But I'm afraid we don't have any left."

"Your receptionist thinks there may be some knocking about in the back of one of your warehouses. She's gone looking."

The man straightened his back. "She's an optimist. There is none left—but I'll go and look for it too."

"Yes, please. I can make do with a very small piece, if it's the right shape. Maybe I should come—"

"No, you can't. Health and safety. Wait here."

Domenico sat back down and waited, his knee rapping against the chair next to his. The old man returned five minutes later. "I'm sorry, there's nothing left. Nothing at all."

Domenico's heart dropped to his stomach. He stood up and pleaded: "I've got a chisel and a hammer in my Vespa's pannier. Could I try and cut a piece out of the disused quarry, if I find one?"

"God forbid, young man! Health and safety and all that, you know… Look: if I were you, I'd try the Greco quarry. They might have some."

Domenico thanked the old man, jumped on his Vespa and accelerated off towards the Greco quarry. Unfortunately, they didn't have any *Albicocca* either, but told him that they could order it and send it to him within the following twenty-four hours. Domenico ordered it, fervently hoping that they would keep their promise.

By the time he got back to the cathedral it was already lunchtime. His cup of coffee was sitting on his worktop, but the thick black liquid had gone stale and cold, despite the extra-thick ceramic walls of the small cup. He poured it down the sink and picked up the cup to return it to the café, where he would buy himself some lunch. On the way out, he checked on the meridian line one more time, hoping against all hopes that the fish might have returned from their swim. It was midday and a beam of sunlight coming through the roof's gnomonic hole shone on the line just where the gouged holes lay. What bad luck. If it had been any other time of year, he could have temporarily filled the holes with other materials without anyone noticing. But now? He might as well console himself with a pizzetta at the café.

***

The next day, no delivery of marble arrived in the morning, nor at lunchtime, or in the afternoon. At 4:55, Domenico rang the Greco quarry.

"I'm sorry, but our usual suppliers have suddenly run out of *Albicocca*. We've had to order it from Tuscany. It should arrive in thirty days," they said.

Domenico groaned. "I need it for tomorrow. Is there anywhere else in Sicily where I can find it? I'm happy to go and get it myself."

"There's only one quarry in the whole of Sicily which has *Albicocca*. They're our suppliers but they've run out."

It must be the Lavigna quarry. If they were the quarry which supplied everyone else with *Albicocca*, why had the old man suggested to him that he asked the Greco quarry? Just to get him off his back? "I see. Thank you anyway."

Domenico slumped in his chair in surrender: there was no way he could reconstruct the missing fish before the Chrism Mass the next day. He sighed, got up and wandered over to his collection of mortar mixtures. He chose a peachy-colored one, mixed it with water and slapped it into the holes until there was no gap. It was an ugly sight—like the way a grey amalgam tooth filling looks compared to a white ceramic one—but at least the soles and heels of tomorrow's churchgoers would not dig further into the holes.

***

The next morning, the incense burners spread their scent through the cathedral's spacious nave, the faithful sang with their cardinal and clergy, and Domenico rang the Lavigna quarry. He asked to speak to the boss.

"Hello, I know that you haven't got any in stock, but I really need some *Albicocca* marble. I only want a small piece, the size of an exercise book. If you really can't find anything lurking in the back of your warehouses, I'm happy to sign any disclaimer you want me to sign, if you let me search your old quarry and chisel any piece I can find."

"I'm sorry, but we cannot let you," replied the boss, unmovable. He cited health and safety regulations, laws, rules, and even an old curse.

But Domenico wouldn't desist. They played tug of war over the phone for half an hour until, exasperated, the man said, "Anyway, fish are not orange: they're silver-grey. I can give you a piece of silver granite, which would look much better."

"No thanks. I need *Albicocca* and nothing else will do," Domenico replied, before finally closing the call.

Giovanni padded over and patted Domenico on the shoulder. "Mass is almost over. Let's go and see how your fish are doing."

Domenico unfolded himself off the chair and followed Giovanni into the empty nave of the cathedral. Song sheets lay messily on the pews and on the floor, but the mortar was still there, intact, protecting the hole.

"There's something to be happy about: your mortar job was a good one. Come and have lunch: it's midday," Giovanni said.

***

Under Domenico and Giovanni's combined weight, the Vespa could barely make it up the hill to the Lavigna quarry. The receptionist betrayed a little surprise at seeing Domenico again, but the biggest surprise was for Domenico, when she let them into Signor Lavigna's office. Yes, because Signor Lavigna was the same old man with the wrinkly face who had told Domenico to ask the Grecos. He invited them to sit down, clearly more out of habit than conviction. Domenico and Giovanni sat down.

"I know you've got something to do with the missing fish. If you decide to tell me everything now, I won't report you to the police. Otherwise, I'll find out by myself and report you," Domenico said, steely-eyed.

"I don't know what you're talking about." Even under his tan, the color drained off the old man's face.

"You told me that grey granite was more appropriate for fish when I had never told you what I needed your marble for."

The man's hands, clasped on his desk, started to shake. He gave a deep sigh and started speaking. "My son wants me to step down and pass the helm of the company to him, but I don't want to retire and spend the rest of my life at home. Last year at Easter, when we were at Mass in the cathedral, he made me promise that I would let him take the lead when the sun of the meridian line fell on the Pisces marker. As the months passed and the day approached, I panicked and thought that, if the *pisces* went off for a 'swim', I could stay put without breaking my promise." He slumped in his chair, looking like a crumpled-up raisin of misery and shame. "I'd heard about you—you have a good reputation, and I thought that you wouldn't repair the Pisces with anything other than the original marble, so I made sure you didn't get any *Albicocca*."

With trembling hands, he reached into his desk drawer and pulled out two fish-shaped pieces of beautiful salmon-pink marble. "Here you are. Time for the fish to go home. I'm sorry."

***

It didn't take Domenico longer than three hours to remove the mortar and insert the fish back into the holes. By the afternoon, the gnomonic hole was unplugged too and, the next day, the sun shone again, cheerful and bright, on Pisces, then, the following month, on Aries and Taurus. When it got to Gemini, Domenico received a letter.

He tore the envelope open absentmindedly and, seeing a glossy brochure inside, was about to toss it into the recycling when a photo attracted his attention. It was the old man from the quarry, Signor Lavigna, posing with a shiny yellow hard hat, while he talked to a group of people, all in hard hats, gathered around a freshly cut slab of beautiful pink marble. The caption read: *Signor Lavigna, explaining the history of the family business and of each type of marble. Book your quarry tour now!*

Domenico smiled. It had been his idea to open up the quarry for tours and for Signor Lavigna to be the brand ambassador when he stepped down from the chairmanship. He then noticed that three pieces of paper had fallen from the envelope. They were two complimentary quarry tour tickets and a note:

Thank you, Domenico, for your excellent suggestion. I am greatly enjoying my new job. Best wishes, Mimmo Lavigna

PS. You'll be glad to hear that I've carried out a thorough health and safety assessment!

15. ONCE BITTEN

Tanino scowled at his wife. The moment their only granddaughter, Valentina, had arrived at their apartment, Melina had whisked her off to the kitchen to bake cookies and then, when the cookies were in the oven, she had got her onto a crochet project. In all this, he hadn't yet managed to get a word in edgeways with Valentina.

"Would anyone like to go out on a bicycle?" he asked, looking hopefully at Valentina, the only bicycle-owner in the room.

"It's about to rain. Valentina will catch a cold," Melina replied for the girl.

Tanino looked out the window. Yes, the sky was black with thunderous clouds but what harm could a little rain do to a strong, healthy girl? Never mind. He waited a little then asked, "Would anyone like to play cards?"

Nobody replied.

"Draughts?" It was his last, hopeless attempt.

Silence.

He consoled himself by thinking that his seven-year-old granddaughter might not even have heard him: her tongue was sticking out of her mouth with the effort of twisting the yarn around the tiny metal hook of her crochet stick. It mystified him how people could turn yarn into clothes with just a hooked stick. It was almost magical. No wonder he was unable to snatch Valentina from her grandmother. Shuffling cards around a table couldn't compete with turning a string into a hat.

"Who's this hat for?" he asked Valentina.

"My doggy."

"You have a doggy now, do you?" Tanino couldn't imagine Valentina's mother allowing a pet in her apartment.

"Oh no, it's only a plush toy," Melina clarified in a tone of relief.

"Don't you like dogs, *Nonna*?" Valentina asked.

"I can't stand them. I was bitten once." Melina began her riveting tale of her first and only encounter with a dog and, again, Tanino felt he had no place in that conversation.

"I'm going out," he announced.

Even if the sky looked leaden, Melina didn't try to stop him: she obviously wasn't worried about him catching a cold.

There were very few customers at the café at this time of day and, as it wasn't Tanino's usual time to visit, he didn't know any of them. As soon as the owner, Carmelo, saw Tanino, he flipped the kitchen towel over his shoulder, rounded the bar and scuttled up to him. "Have you heard, Tanino?"

"Heard what?"

"About poor Enzo. He passed away last night," Carmelo whispered, crossing himself.

"No!" Tanino put down his coffee and crossed himself too.

"Yes."

They kept a respectful silence for a few moments, then Tanino asked, "How did it happen?"

"Nobody knows. He was in the apartment with his dog. The poor animal barked and alerted the neighbors, but they didn't make it in time."

"Poor Enzo."

"And poor dog, too. For now, the neighbors are looking after him, but they can't keep him. Do you know anyone who would like to adopt a sweet old mongrel?"

Tanino thought about it. "No."

"I would have him, but I can't keep a dog in a shop full of sausage rolls, ham pizzas and beef *arancine*. He's such a lovely dog, though—" Carmelo stopped, as if an idea had suddenly crossed his mind. "Why don't you have him?"

Tanino burst into laughter. "Melina hates dogs with a passion. If a dog came into our home, she would leave."

Carmelo stroked his chin. "How about your granddaughter? I don't know a child who doesn't dream of having a puppy. This dog has long passed his puppy years but he's not much bigger than one."

Tanino drained his coffee and got up from the little table. "It's impossible. Her mother, our daughter, has inherited every drop of Melina's dislike for dogs."

"But what about the girl?"

"She would give an arm and leg to have a dog, I'm sure, but that's not the point."

"Then take him home, have a try. He's such a nice fella that I'm sure the women will fall in love with him." Carmelo sat down at the table and put a hand on Tanino's arm, so he sat down again.

Melina would be furious if he brought home a dog, but perhaps she deserved it, after she had shot down every one of his attempts to connect with Valentina. Tanino could just picture Valentina's face when he brought home the dog, and he could imagine walking the dog with Valentina without Melina. Because there was no way Melina would dream of hijacking or gate-crashing the dog-walking or any of their activities with the dog. No matter how many cakes and crochet hats Melina offered, she couldn't give Valentina time with a dog! Tanino smiled under his moustache.

"Alright. We'll try," Tanino said. "But now I desperately need another coffee."

"Good boy!" Carmelo clapped his hands together and floated back behind the bar.

***

"We're home!" Tanino called from the door.

We? It couldn't be Valentina's mother: it was too early. Who could be accompanying Tanino? Melina ran a hand through her hair to plump it up and smoothed her skirt. Then a noise froze her blood: it was that tic-tic-tic noise that animals' claws make on a hard floor. She felt her jaw tense and was sure that the hair on her head didn't need plumping up anymore. It *couldn't* be a dog: Tanino knew not to invite a dog-owner into their apartment. But when her husband appeared on the threshold, this was precisely the situation: there was a dog at the end of the lead in his hand. Not only was there a dog in the house, but its owner was missing.

"I've found an old 'puppy' who needs a little girl to look after him," Tanino announced, looking at Valentina. "Any volunteers?"

Melina's skin broke into goose bumps and her eyes bulged out of her skull when Valentina squealed, "Me!" and thrust her hand up in the air.

"No way!" Melina croaked. How could her grandchild not be terrified of a carnivore with fangs and claws?

Tanino's tale of the dog's gallant attempt to rescue his owner didn't change Melina's attitude: this dog was not a hero in need of a new home but a wolf in disguise. So, when Tanino and Valentina took him for a walk, Melina refused to accompany them. Instead, she waited impatiently at home until Valentina's mum came to pick up her daughter. Reassuringly, she reacted to the dog news just as Melina had. Ah, at least someone in the family saw sense, Melina thought. And that was good news: if the dog was not welcome in either of their homes, he would have to go.

***

"What are we going to do, *Nonno*?" Valentina asked Tanino when it became obvious that no amount of begging or cajoling would change *Nonna* or *Mamma*'s refusal to keep 'Bello'—as Valentina had called him.

Tanino's heart squeezed. He had seen the light in Valentina's eyes when she first saw the dog. He had seen her stroke him tenderly and scoop up his poop from the pavement without recoiling. How could he part Valentina from him? Even if they decided to 'return' him, whom to? Neither Carmelo nor Enzo's neighbors could keep him. Tanino heaved a sigh and looked despondently at the girl and the sweet old dog. Then he gasped.

"I have an idea!"

***

Melina had been immensely relieved when Tanino had taken the dog to his brother's apartment. Even there, the carnivore was a bit too close for comfort for her, and his presence there meant that she wouldn't visit her sister-in-law for the time being. But it was certainly better than having him at home.

However, as the days went by, Melina started to regret the fact that Valentina and Tanino spent a lot of time away together at his brother's house. Since the dog had tumbled into their lives, she hardly ever saw her grandchild anymore. She could only imagine her cuddling up to the fanged creature, Tanino holding her hand to show her where it might be safe to stroke this wild hound, the two of them bonding as they risked life and limb together.

It was so unbearable that, one day, Melina decided to go and visit her sister-in-law just after Tanino and Valentina had left home.

"Hello, Melina!" Fina looked just as surprised to see Melina as Melina was to be there. "Tanino and Valentina should be here soon, I believe. I'm not sure if you want to come in…" Fina looked uncomfortable, "…because the dog is here."

Melina harrumphed. Just then, Bello limped into the entrance hall and looked at her, wagging his tail. Melina's muscles tensed. The dog advanced a little further, then slowly lowered himself into a sitting position by Fina's feet. For the first time, Melina observed him with interest rather than fear. From his limp, his white muzzle and his slow movements, she could tell that he was an old dog and felt a rush of sympathy. Maybe she shouldn't be afraid of a little old creature like him. She slowly bent down and gingerly stretched her hand over his head. He didn't try to bite her. She stroked the top of his head. It felt softer and cleaner than she had expected. She could almost hear Fina holding her breath in surprise. Just then, the elevator stopped on the landing behind her and the door opened.

"*Nonna*! Bello!" Valentina shot out of the elevator and the dog barked with excitement, almost in Melina's face. And she almost fainted.

***

Tanino would have been surprised enough to see Melina at his brother's place, let alone find her patting Bello's head. But Valentina didn't seem even a little surprised. Instead, she set off teaching Melina to tickle Bello under his chin and on his belly. It was a sight Tanino hadn't thought he would ever see. Neither did he expect Melina to join them as they took Bello for a walk, nor was he prepared to hear her say gingerly to Fina, "We could try keeping the dog in our apartment if you are tired of looking after him."

Fina glanced at Tanino as if to check how she should reply, then she said that yes, she did find it a bit tiring and she would be grateful if they took him with them.

***

Days went by and, when Valentina was at school and Tanino at the café giving his friends the latest account of the dog's heroic deeds, Melina was no longer alone at home. Somebody now looked lovingly at her from his basket while she did the housework, sat by her feet when she did her crochet and followed her around the house.

When it was time to go out to the baker's and buy the bread for lunch, Melina would change his collar to a velvet one with a bow and diamond studs, she would brush him with a special brush, and in the sweetest voice, say to him, "Time for our walk, *Bellissimo*."

ABOUT THE AUTHOR

Best known as The Sicilian Mama, Stefania was born in Sicily and immediately started growing, but not very much.

She left her sunny island after falling head over heels in love with an Englishman, and now she lives in the UK with her husband and their three children.

Having finally learnt English, she's enjoying it so much that she now writes short stories and romance novels. Her short stories have been longlisted for the Mogford Prize for Food and Drink Writing, commended by the Society of Medical Authors, and won other prizes, but what she likes most is to hear from her readers. If you have enjoyed her stories, she'd love you to leave a review on Amazon or Goodreads or contact her through her website:

www.stefaniahartley.com

Or Facebook: www.facebook.com/StefaniaHartley

Or Twitter: @TheSicilianMama

If you sign up for her newsletter:

www.stefaniahartley.com/subscribe

she'll send you an exclusive free copy of her short story *Not a Speck of Dust* and let you know when she's releasing a new book. Out now:

A SLIP OF THE TONGUE

Printed in Poland
by Amazon Fulfillment
Poland Sp. z o.o., Wrocław